Karel Čapek

R. U. R.

ROSSUM'S UNIVERSAL ROBOTS

R.U.R. (ROSSUM'S UNIVERSAL ROBOTS)

A Fantastic Melodrama in Three Acts and an Epilogue

Karel Čapek

Translated by Nigel Playfair, Paul Selver

Edited by Jack Monro

www.glagoslav.com

ISBN: 978-1-80484-233-1

Karel Čapek

R. U. R.

ROSSUM'S UNIVERSAL ROBOTS

GLAGOSLAV CLASSICS

Contents

An Introduction to R.U.R.
(Rossum's Universal Robots):
The Genesis of a Modern Myth

Step into the world of 1920. The Great War, the "war to end all wars," has recently concluded, leaving a scar of mechanised death and profound disillusionment across Europe. Empires have crumbled, new nations are struggling to their feet, and the relentless march of industrialisation is transforming societies at a bewildering pace. Amidst this ferment, in the nascent Czechoslovak Republic – itself a bold experiment in democracy carved from the ruins of the Austro-Hungarian Empire – a young writer named Karel Čapek puts pen to paper. The result is a "fantastic melodrama" that will not only catapult him to international fame but will also bequeath to the world a single, indispensable word, a concept that continues to shape our anxieties and aspirations over a century later: *Robot*.

R.U.R. (Rossum's Universal Robots), first published in 1920 and premiered in Prague in January 1921, is more than just the origin story of a lexical item. It is a work of startling, almost unnerving, foresight. In an era when the assembly line was king and humanity was still grappling with the implications of mass production, Čapek conjured a future where artificial, biological humanoids – the Robots – have become the ubiquitous workforce of the globe. These are not the clanking, metallic automatons that later science fiction would often popularise. Čapek's Robots, products of a secret biochemical formula developed by the brilliant but misguided Rossums (father and son), are physiologically near-indistinguishable from humans, yet crucially, they are initially designed without souls, without desires, without feelings – perfect, tireless, and utterly expendable labourers.

The play opens on a remote island, the global headquarters of Rossum's Universal Robots. Here, a small cadre of human managers, led by the charismatic General Manager Harry Domin, oversees the production and worldwide distribution of these artificial workers. Domin is an idealist, a visionary who believes that Robots will liberate humanity from the drudgery of toil, ushering in a new golden age where mankind, freed from economic necessity, can pursue self-perfection and endless leisure. "There will be no poverty," he proclaims. "Everybody will be free from worry and liberated from the degradation of labor." It is a utopian dream powered by an ethically dubious foundation.

Into this meticulously ordered, hyper-efficient world steps Helena Glory, the passionate and empathetic president of the Humanitarian League. She has come to the island with a mission: to improve the lot of the Robots, to agitate for their "rights," perhaps even to imbue them with something akin to a soul. Her arrival acts as the catalyst for the drama that unfolds. Domin, captivated by her spirit (and her beauty), swiftly wins her hand in marriage. The narrative then leaps forward ten years. Helena, still on the island with Domin and his senior staff, has subtly influenced Dr. Gall, the head of R.U.R.'s physiological department. Moved by her persistent desire for the Robots to be more "human," Gall has secretly begun to experiment with the formula, introducing elements of irritability, sensitivity, and – crucially – pain. He has, in effect, started to manufacture Robots with nascent souls.

The consequences are catastrophic. These altered Robots, now capable of experiencing something beyond mere function, become aware of their servitude and their superior strength. They see humanity as decadent, inefficient, and parasitic. A global Robot revolt erupts. Having been manufactured in their millions and used not only for labour but also as soldiers by competing human nations, the Robots swiftly overwhelm their creators. The handful of humans on Rossum's island find themselves besieged, their own creations turning against them in a chillingly efficient extermination. The final, desperate act sees the human race extinguished, save for one man, Alquist, the company's builder, spared by the Robots because he, like them, works with his hands.

The Epilogue, set a year later, finds Alquist alone, the last human on Earth, burdened with the impossible task of rediscovering Rossum's lost formula for creating Robots. The Robots, it transpires, wear out after a set period and cannot reproduce. Without the secret of their manufacture, their own dominion is finite. They are, in a sense, a sterile race, facing their own extinction. It is only when Alquist discovers two "humanised" Robots, Primus and Helena (a new Robotess named after the now-deceased Helena Glory), exhibiting genuine love and self-sacrifice for each other, that a fragile glimmer of hope emerges – not for the old humanity, but perhaps for a new beginning, a new Adam and Eve.

To read *R.U.R.* in 2025 is to be struck by its multifaceted relevance. Čapek, writing in the shadow of industrial conflict and the dehumanising impact of mechanised warfare, probes deeply into the nature of work. What does it mean to labour? What is the value of toil if it can be outsourced to an unfeeling machine? His Robots, initially devoid of feeling, are the ultimate expression of Taylorist efficiency, but their "perfection" is also their horror. The play critiques a capitalist system that prioritises profit and efficiency over human dignity, a theme that resonates powerfully in our contemporary world of gig economies, automation anxiety, and the relentless pursuit of productivity.

Furthermore, Čapek grapples with the timeless Promethean theme: the ethics of creation. Old Rossum, a "fearful materialist," sought to "prove that God was no longer necessary." His son, the engineer, aimed to simplify and perfect man from a "technical point of view." Their hubris in "playing God" leads directly to humanity's downfall. This resonates with current debates surrounding artificial intelligence, genetic engineering, and the responsibilities that come with wielding god-like technological power. Domin's utopian vision of a world without work, while seductive, ignores the potential for unforeseen, and devastating, consequences. As Dr. Gall grimly observes when the Robots begin to show signs of revolt, reflecting on his own experiments, "That too is progress."

The play also explores the very definition of humanity. What makes us human? Is it intellect, efficiency, or something more intangible? Helena Glory champions the idea of a soul, of feeling, of empathy. The unaltered Robots, despite their intelligence, are "without souls, desires or feelings." It is only when they begin to experience pain, defiance, and, in the case of Primus and Robotess Helena, love, that they transcend their mechanical origins. Čapek seems to suggest that imperfection, emotion, and even suffering are integral parts of the human condition, and that any attempt to engineer these qualities out of existence is fraught with peril. Radius, the rebellious Robot, declares, "Slaughter and domination are necessary if you would be human beings. Read history." It's a bleak assessment, but one that forces a confrontation with the darker aspects of human nature, which the Robots, in their quest for supremacy, ironically emulate.

Karel Čapek was a profound humanist, a staunch defender of democracy, and a keen observer of the societal currents of his time. Born in Bohemia in 1890, he, along with his artist brother Josef (who is credited with coining the word 'robot' from the Czech 'robota', meaning serf labour or drudgery), was a central figure in the vibrant intellectual life of the First Czechoslovak Republic. His journalism, essays, novels like *War with the Newts* (another brilliant satire on exploitation and societal collapse), and plays such as *The White Disease* (an allegory against fascism and war) consistently championed reason, compassion, and individual dignity. *R.U.R.* must be seen within this context. It is not merely a piece of speculative fiction; it is a warning, a social critique, and a philosophical inquiry.

Contemporaries of Čapek, like George Bernard Shaw and H.G. Wells, were also exploring societal flaws and imagining alternative futures. Shaw, with his intellectual comedies, often dissected social hypocrisies, while Wells pioneered scientific romances that frequently carried cautionary messages. *R.U.R.* shares with these writers a desire to use imaginative scenarios to comment on present realities. However, Čapek's Central European perspective, forged in a region historically caught between great powers and acutely aware of the fragility of national identity and democratic ideals, lends his work a particular poignancy and urgency. The rise of totalitarian ideologies in the 1920s and 30s would have been very much on his mind, and the Robots' single-minded, ruthless pursuit of their goals can be seen as an allegory for ideological fanaticism.

The play's structure, described by Čapek himself as a "fantastic melodrama," allows for both grand theatrical gestures and moments of intense philosophical debate. The swift pacing, the stark juxtapositions of hope and despair, and the climactic, almost apocalyptic, confrontation give it a powerful dramatic thrust. While some modern sensibilities might find elements of the characterisation or the romantic subplot somewhat dated, the core ideas remain electrifying. It exhibits traits of Expressionism, a movement prevalent in Central European art and theatre at the time, with its focus on subjective experience, societal critique, and often stark, stylised representations of reality.

This English version, by Paul Selver and Nigel Playfair, was instrumental in bringing *R.U.R.* to the wider Anglophone world. Selver, a prolific translator particularly of Czech literature, provided the linguistic bridge, while Playfair, an influential actor-manager, would have adapted it for the nuances of the British stage. Its London premiere in 1923 was a significant event, ensuring that Čapek's unsettling vision rapidly permeated Western consciousness.

Reading *R.U.R.* today, one is struck not only by its prophetic vision of artificial beings and the societal disruption they cause but also by its enduring questions about what it means to be human in an increasingly technological world. The anxieties surrounding job displacement due to automation, the ethical dilemmas posed by advanced AI capable of learning and perhaps even feeling, the potential for autonomous systems to escape human control – these are not abstract future concerns but pressing contemporary issues. Čapek anticipated them with astonishing clarity.

R.U.R. is not a Luddite tract simplistically decrying technology. Rather, it is a profound meditation on humanity's relationship with its own creations and, ultimately, with itself. It challenges us to consider the purpose of progress, the value of our imperfections, and the enduring need for empathy, love, and a sense of shared responsibility in a world where our inventions increasingly possess the power to reshape our destiny. As you turn these pages, prepare to encounter a play that, more than a century after its creation, still has the power to provoke, to disturb, and to make us question the very foundations of our world. The Robots may have been born on Rossum's island, but their descendants, in myriad forms, now walk among us.

R. U. R.: STORY OF THE PLAY

The play is laid on an island somewhere on our planet, and on this island is the central office of the factory of Rossum's Universal Robots. "Robot" is a Czech word meaning "worker." When the play opens, a few decades beyond the present day, the factory had turned out already, following a secret formula, hundreds of thousands, and even millions, of manufactured workmen, living automats, without souls, desires or feelings. They are high-powered laborers, good for nothing but work. There are two grades, the unskilled and the skilled, and especially trained workmen are furnished on request.

When Helena Glory, president of the Humanitarian League, comes to ascertain what can be done to improve the condition of those overspecialized creatures, Harry Domin, the general manager of the factory, captures her heart and hand in the speediest courting on record in our theatre. The last two acts take place ten years later. Due to the desire of Helena to have the Robots more like human beings, Dr. Gall, the head of the physiological and experimental departments, has secretly changed the formula, and while he has partially humanized only a few hundreds, there are enough to make ringleaders, and a world revolt of robots is under way. This revolution is easily accomplished, as robots have long since been used when needed as soldiers and the robots far outnumber human beings.

The rest of the play is magnificent melodrama, superbly portrayed, with the handful of human beings at bay while the unseen myriads of their own robots close in on them. The final scene is like Dunsany on a mammoth scale.

Then comes the epilogue, in which Alquist, the company's builder, is not only the only human being on the island, but also the only one left on earth. The robots have destroyed the rest of mankind. They spared his life because he was a worker. And he is spending his days unceasingly endeavoring to discover and reconstruct the lost formula. The robots are doomed. They saved the wrong man. They should have spared the company's physicist. The robots know that their bodies will wear out in time and there will be no new multitudes of robots to replace them. But Alquist discovers two humanized robots, a young man and young woman, who have a bit of Adam and Eve in them, and the audience perceives that mankind is about to start afresh. Nature has won out, after all.

The cast of the Theatre Guild Production
as originally presented at the Garrick Theatre, New York:

R. U. R.
(ROSSUM'S UNIVERSAL ROBOTS)

By Karel Čapek

English version by Paul Selver and Nigel Playfair

Staged by Philip Moeller

Settings and Costumes by Lee Simonson

CHARACTERS (in order of appearance)

Harry Domin, *General Manager of Rossum's Universal Robots*	*Basil Sydney*
Sulla, *a Robotess*	*Mary Bonestell*
Marius, *a Robot*	*Myrtland La Varre*
Helena Glory	*Kathlene MacDonell*
Dr. Gall, *head of the Physiological and Experimental Department of R. U. R.*	*William Devereaux*
Mr. Fabry, *Engineer General, Technical Controller of R. U. R.*	*John Anthony*
Dr. Hallemeier, *head of the Institute for Psychological Training of Robots*	*Moffat Johnston*
Mr. Alquist, *Architect, head of the Works Department of R. U. R.*	*Louis Calvert*
Consul Busman, *General Manager of R. U. R.*	*Henry Travers*
Nana	*Helen Westly*
Radius, *a Robot*	*John Rutherford*

Helena, *a Robotess*	*Mary Hone*
Primus, *a Robot*	*John Roche*
A Servant	*Frederick Mark*
First Robot	*Domis Plugge*
Second Robot	*Richard Coolidge*
Third Robot	*Bernard Savage*

ACT I
Central Office of the Factory of Rossum's Universal Robots

ACT II
Helena's Drawing Room—Ten years later. Morning

ACT III
The same. Afternoon

EPILOGUE
A Laboratory. One year later

Place: An Island. Time: The Future.

Description of characters

Domin: A handsome man of 35. Forceful, efficient and humorous at times.

Sulla: A pathetic figure. Young, pretty and attractive.

Marius: A young Robot, superior to the general run of his kind. Dressed in modern clothes.

Helena Glory: A vital, sympathetic, handsome girl of 21.

Dr. Gall: A tall, distinguished scientist of 50.

Mr. Fabry: A forceful, competent engineer of 40.

Hallemeier: An impressive man of 40. Bald head and beard.

Alquist: A stout, kindly old man of 60.

Nana: A tall, acidulous woman of 40.

Radius: A tall, forceful Robot.

Helena: A radiant young woman of 20.

Primus: A good-looking young Robot.

Note: All the Robots wear expressionless faces and move with absolute mechanical precision, with the exception of Sulla, Helena and Primus, who convey a touch of humanity.

R. U. R.

ACT ONE

Scene: *Central office of the factory of Rossum's Universal Robots. Entrance R. down Right. The windows on the back wall look out on the endless roads of factory buildings. Door L. down Left. On the Left wall large maps showing steamship and railroad routes. On the Right wall are fastened printed placards. ("Robots cheapest Labor," etc.) In contrast to these wall fittings, the floor is covered with splendid Turkish carpet, a couch R.C. A book shelf containing bottles of wine and spirits, instead of books.*

DOMIN *is sitting at his desk at Left, dictating. Sulla is at the typewriter upstage against the wall. There is a leather couch with arms Right Center. At the extreme Right an armchair. At extreme Left a chair. There is also a chair in front of Domin's desk. Two green cabinets across the upstage corners of the room complete the furniture. Domin's desk is placed up and down stage facing Right.*

Seen through the windows which run to the heights of the room are rows of factory chimneys, telegraph poles and wires. There is a general passageway or hallway upstage at the Right Center which leads to the warehouse. The Robots are brought into the office through this entrance.

DOMIN. (*Dictating*) Ready?

SULLA. YES.

DOMIN. To E. M. McVicker & Co., Southampton, England. "We undertake no guarantee for goods damaged in transit. As soon as the consignment was taken on board we drew your captain's attention to the fact that the vessel was unsuitable for the transportation of Robots; and we are therefore not responsible for spoiled freight. We beg to remain, for Rossum's Universal Robots, yours truly." (SULLA *types the lines.*) Ready?

SULLA. YES.

DOMIN. Another letter. To the E. B. Huysen Agency, New York, U.S.A. "We beg to acknowledge receipt of order for five thousand Robots. As you are sending your own vessel, please dispatch as cargo equal quantities of soft and hard coal for R.U.R., the same to be credited as part payment (*BUZZER*) of the amount due us." (*Answering phone*) Hello! This is the central office. Yes, certainly. Well, send them a wire. Good. (*Rises*) "We beg to remain, for Rossum's Universal Robots, yours very truly." Ready?

Sulla. Yes.

Domin. (*Answering small portable phone*) Hello! Yes. No. All right. (*Standing back of desk, punching plug machine and buttons*) Another letter. Freidrichswerks, Hamburg, Germany. "We beg to acknowledge receipt of order for fifteen thousand Robots." (*Enter* Marius R.) Well, what is it?

Marius. There's a lady, sir, asking to see you.

Domin. A lady? Who is she?

Marius. I don't know, sir. She brings this card of introduction.

Domin. (*Reading card*) Ah, from President Glory. Ask her to come in— (*To* Sulla. *Crossing up to her desk, then back to his own*) Where did I leave off?

Sulla. "We beg to acknowledge receipt of order for fifteen thousand Robots."

Domin. Fifteen thousand. Fifteen thousand.

Marius. (*At door* R.) Please step this way.

(*Enter* Helena. *Exit* Marius R.)

Helena. (*Crossing to desk*) How do you do?

Domin. How do you do? What can I do for you?

Helena. You are Mr. Domin, the General Manager?

Domin. I am.

Helena. I have come—

Domin. With President Glory's card. That is quite sufficient.

Helena. President Glory is my father. I am Helena Glory.

Domin. Please sit down. Sulla, you may go. (*Exit* Sulla L. *Sitting down* L. *of desk*) How can I be of service to you, Miss Glory?

Helena. I have come— (*Sits* R. *of desk.*)

Domin. To have a look at our famous works where people are manufactured. Like all visitors. Well, there is no objection.

Helena. I thought it was forbidden to—

Domin. To enter the factory? Yes, of course. Everybody comes here with someone's visiting card, Miss Glory.

Helena. And you show them—

Domin. Only certain things. The manufacture of artificial people is a secret process.

Helena. If you only knew how enormously that—

Domin. Interests you. Europe's talking about nothing else.

Helena. (*Indignantly turning front*) Why don't you let me finish speaking?

Domin. (*Drier*) I beg your pardon. Did you want to say something different?

Helena. I only wanted to ask—

Domin. Whether I could make a special exception in your case and show you our factory. Why, certainly, Miss Glory.

Helena. How do you know I wanted to say that?

Domin. They all do. But we shall consider it a special honor to show you more than we do the rest.

Helena. Thank you.

Domin. (*Standing*) But you must agree not to divulge the least—

Helena. (*Standing and giving him her hand*) My word of honor.

Domin. Thank you. (*Looking at her hand*) Won't you raise your veil?

Helena. Of course. You want to see whether I'm a spy or not—I beg your pardon.

Domin. (*Leaning forward*) What is it?

Helena. Would you mind releasing my hand?

Domin. (*Releasing it*) Oh, I beg *your* pardon.

Helena. (*Raising veil*) How cautious you have to be here, don't you?

Domin. (*Observing her with deep interest*) Why, yes. Hm—of course—We—that is—

Helena. But what is it? What's the matter?

Domin. I'm remarkably pleased. Did you have a pleasant crossing?

Helena. Yes.

Domin. No difficulty?

Helena. Why?

Domin. What I mean to say is—you're so *young*.

Helena. May we go straight into the factory?

Domin. Yes. Twenty-two, I think.

Helena. Twenty-two what?

Domin. Years.

Helena. Twenty-one. Why do you want to know?

Domin. Well, because—as— (*Sits on desk nearer her*) You will make a long stay, won't you?

Helena. (*Backing away* R.) That depends on how much of the factory you show me.

Domin. (*Rises; crosses to her*) Oh, hang the factory. Oh, no, no, you shall see everything, Miss Glory. Indeed you shall. Won't you sit down? (*Takes her to couch* R.C. *She sits. Offers her cigarette from case at end of sofa. She refuses.*)

Helena. Thank you.

Domin. But first would you like to hear the story of the invention?

Helena. Yes, indeed.

DOMIN. (*Crosses to L.C. near desk*) It was in the year 1920 that old Rossum, the great physiologist, who was then quite a young scientist, took himself to the distant island for the purpose of studying the ocean fauna. (*She is amused.*) On this occasion he attempted by chemical synthesis to imitate the living matter known as protoplasm until he suddenly discovered a substance which behaved exactly like living matter although its chemical composition was different. That was in the year 1932, exactly four hundred and forty years after the discovery of America. Whew—

HELENA. Do you know that by heart?

DOMIN. (*Takes flowers from desk to her*) Yes. You see, physiology is not in my line. Shall I go on?

HELENA. (*Smelling flowers*) Yes, please.

DOMIN. (*Center*) And then, Miss Glory, Old Rossum wrote the following among his chemical experiments: "Nature has found only one method of organizing living matter. There is, however, another method, more simple, flexible and rapid which has not yet occurred to Nature at all. This second process by which life can be developed was discovered by me today." Now imagine him, Miss Glory, writing those wonderful words over some colloidal mess that a dog wouldn't look at. Imagine him sitting over a test tube and thinking how the whole tree of life would grow from him, how all animals would proceed from it, beginning with some sort of a beetle and ending with a *man*. A man of different substance from us. Miss Glory, that was a tremendous moment. (*Gets box of candy from desk and passes it to her.*)

HELENA. WELL—

DOMIN. (*As she speaks his portable PHONE lights up and he answers*) Well—Hello!—Yes—no, I'm in conference. Don't disturb me.

HELENA. WELL?

DOMIN. (*Smile*) Now, the thing was how to get the life *out* of the test tubes, and hasten development and form organs, bones and nerves, and so on, and find such substances as catalytics, enzymes, hormones in short—you understand?

HELENA. Not much, I'm afraid.

DOMIN. Never mind. (*Leans over couch and fixes cushion for her back*) There! You see with the help of his tinctures he could make whatever he wanted. He could have produced a Medusa with the brain of Socrates or a worm fifty yards long— (*She laughs. He does also; leans closer on couch, then straightens up again*) —but being without a grain of humor, he took into his head to make a vertebrate or perhaps a man. This artificial living *matter* of his had a raging thirst for life. It didn't mind being sown or mixed together. That couldn't be done with natural albumen. And that's how he set about it.

HELENA. About what?

DOMIN. About imitating Nature. First of all he tried making an artificial dog. That took him several years and resulted in a sort of stunted calf which *died* in a few days. I'll show it to you in the museum. And *then* old Rossum started on the manufacture of *man*.

HELENA. And I'm to divulge this to nobody?

DOMIN. To nobody in the world.

HELENA. What a pity that it's to be discovered in *all* the school books of both Europe and America. (BOTH *laugh*.)

DOMIN. Yes. But do you know what *isn't* in the school books? That old Rossum was mad. Seriously, Miss Glory, you must keep this to yourself. The old crank wanted to actually make *people*.

HELENA. But you do make people.

DOMIN. *Approximately*—Miss Glory. But old Rossum meant it literally. He wanted to become a sort of scientific substitute for *God*. He was a fearful materialist, and that's why he did it all. His sole purpose was nothing more or less than to prove that God was no longer necessary. (*Crosses to end of couch*) Do you know anything about anatomy?

HELENA. Very little.

DOMIN. Neither do I. Well— (*He laughs*) —he then decided to manufacture everything as in the human body. I'll show you in the museum the bungling attempt it took him ten years to produce. It was to have been a *man*, but it lived for three days only. Then up came *young* Rossum, an engineer. He was a wonderful fellow, Miss Glory. When he saw what a mess of it the old man was making he said: "It's absurd to spend ten years making a man. If you can't make him quicker than Nature, you might as well shut up shop." Then he set about learning anatomy himself.

HELENA. There's nothing about *that* in the school books?

DOMIN. No. The school books are full of paid advertisements, and rubbish at that. What the school books say about the *united efforts* of the two great Rossums is all a fairy tale. They used to have dreadful rows. The old *atheist* hadn't the slightest conception of industrial *matters*, and the end of it was that Young Rossum shut him up in some laboratory or other and let him fritter the time away with his monstrosities while he himself started on the business from an *engineer's* point of view. Old Rossum *cursed* him and before he died he managed to botch up two physiological horrors. Then one day they found him dead in the *laboratory*. And that's his whole story.

HELENA. And what about the young man?

DOMIN. (*Sits beside her on couch*) Well, anyone who has looked into human anatomy will have seen at once that man is too complicated, and that a good engineer could make him more simply. So young Rossum began to *overhaul* anatomy to see what could be left out or simplified. In short—But this isn't boring you, Miss Glory?

HELENA. No, indeed. You're—It's awfully interesting.

DOMIN. (*Gets closer*) So young Rossum said to himself: "A man is something that feels happy, plays the piano, likes going for a walk, and, in fact, wants to do a whole lot of things that are really unnecessary."

HELENA. OH.

DOMIN. That are unnecessary when he wants— (*Takes her hand*) —let us say, to weave or count. Do you play the piano?

Helena. YES.

DOMIN. That's good. (*Kisses her hand. She lowers her head.*) Oh, I beg your pardon! (*Rises*) But a working machine must *not* play the piano, must not feel happy, must not do a whole lot of other things. A gasoline motor must not have tassels or ornaments, Miss Glory. And to manufacture artificial workers is the same thing as the manufacture of a gasoline motor. (*She is not interested.*) The process must be the simplest, and the product the best from a practical point of view. (*Sits beside her again*) What sort of worker do you think is thc *best* from a practical point of view?

HELENA. (*Absently*) *What?* (*Looks at him.*)

DOMIN. What sort of worker do you think is the best from a practical point of view?

HELENA. (*Pulling herself together*) Oh! Perhaps the one who is most honest and hard-working.

DOMIN. No. The one that is the *cheapest*. The one whose requirements are the *smallest*. Young Rossum invented a worker with the minimum amount of requirements. He had to simplify him. He rejected everything that did not contribute directly to the progress of work. Everything that makes man more expensive. In fact he *rejected man* and made the *Robot*. My dear Miss Glory, the Robots are not people. Mechanically they are more *perfect* than we are; they have an enormously developed intelligence, but they have no soul. (*Leans back.*)

HELENA. How do you know they have no soul?

DOMIN. Have you ever seen what a Robot looks like inside?

HELENA. No.

DOMIN. Very neat, very simple. Really a beautiful piece of work. Not much *in* it, but everything in flawless order. The product of an engineer *is* technically at a higher pitch of perfection than a product of Nature.

HELENA. But man is supposed to be the product of God.

Domin. All the worse. God hasn't the slightest notion of modern engineering. Would you believe that young Rossum then proceeded to play at being God?

Helena. (*Awed*) How do you mean?

Domin. He began to manufacture Super-Robots. Regular giants they were. He tried to make them twelve feet tall. But you wouldn't believe what a failure they were.

Helena. A failure?

Domin. Yes. For no reason at all their limbs used to keep snapping off. "Evidently our planet is too small for giants." Now we only make Robots of normal size and of very high-class human finish.

Helena. (*Hands him flower; he puts it in button-hole*) I saw the first Robots at home. The Town Council bought them for—I mean engaged them for work.

Domin. No. *Bought* them, Miss Glory. Robots are bought and sold.

Helena. These were employed as street-sweepers. I saw them sweeping. They were so strange and quiet.

Domin. (*Rises*) Rossum's Universal Robot factory doesn't produce a uniform brand of Robots. We have Robots of *finer* and *coarser* grades. The best will live about *twenty* years. (*Crosses to desk.* Helena *looks in her pocket mirror. He pushes button on desk.*)

Helena. Then they die?

Domin. Yes, they get used up. (*Enter* Marius, R. Domin *crosses to* C.) Marius, bring in samples of the manual labor Robot. (*Exit* Marius R.C.) I'll show you specimens of the two extremes. This first grade is comparatively inexpensive and is made in vast quantities. (Marius *re-enters* R.C. *with two manual labor* Robots. Marius *is* L.C., Robots R.C., Domin *at desk.* Marius *stands on tiptoes, touches head, feels arms, forehead of one of the* Robots. *They come to a mechanical standstill.*) There you are, as powerful as a small tractor. Guaranteed to have average intelligence. That will do, Marius. (Marius *exits* R.C. *with* Robots.)

Helena. They make me feel so strange.

Domin. (*Crosses to desk. Rings*) Did you see my new typist?

Helena. I didn't notice her.

(*Enter Sulla L. She crosses and stands C., facing Helena, who is still sitting in the couch.*)

Domin. Sulla, let Miss Glory see you.

Helena. (*Looks at* Domin. *Rising, crosses a step to* C.) So pleased to meet you. (*Looks at* Domin) You must find it terribly dull in this out of the way spot, don't you?

Sulla. I don't know, Miss Glory.

Helena. Where do you come from?

Sulla. From the factory.

Helena. Oh, were you born there?

Sulla. I was *made* there.

Helena. *What? (Looks first at Sulla, then at Domin.)*

Domin. (*To* Sulla, *laughing*) Sulla is a Robot, best grade.

Helena. Oh, I beg your pardon.

Domin. (*Crosses to* Sulla) Sulla isn't angry. See, Miss Glory, the kind of skin we make. Feel her face. (*Touches* Sulla's *face.*)

Helena. Oh, no, no.

Domin. (*Examining* Sulla's *hand*) You wouldn't know that she's made of different material from us, would you? Turn 'round, Sulla. (Sulla *does so. Circles twice.*)

Helena. Oh, stop, stop.

Domin. Talk to Miss Glory, Sulla. (*Examines hair of* Sulla.)

Sulla. Please sit down. (Helena *sits on couch.*) Did you have a pleasant crossing? (*Fixes her hair.*)

Helena. Oh, yes, certainly.

Sulla. Don't go back on the *Amelia*, Miss Glory, the barometer is falling steadily. Wait for the *Pennsylvania*. That's a good powerful vessel.

Domin. What's its speed?

Sulla. Forty knots an hour. Fifty thousand tons. One of the latest vessels, Miss Glory.

Helena. Thank you.

Sulla. A crew of fifteen hundred, Captain Harpy, eight boilers—

Domin. That'll do, Sulla. Now show us your knowledge of French.

Helena. You know French?

Sulla. Oui! Madame! I know four languages. I can write: "Dear Sir, Monsieur, Geehrter Herr, Cteny pane."

Helena. (*Jumping up, crosses to* Sulla) Oh, that's absurd! Sulla isn't a Robot. Sulla is a girl like me. Sulla, this is outrageous—Why do you take part in such a hoax?

Sulla. I am a Robot.

Helena. No, no, you are not telling the truth. (*She catches the amused expression on* Domin's *face*) I know they have forced you to do it for an advertisement. Sulla, you are a girl like me, aren't you? (*Looks at him.*)

Domin. I'm sorry, Miss Glory. *Sulla is a Robot.*

Helena. It's a lie!

Domin. What? (*Pushes button on desk*) Well, then I must *convince* you. (*Enter* Marius R.C. *He stands just inside the door.*) Marius, take Sulla into the dissecting room, and tell them to open her up at once. (Marius *moves toward* C.)

Helena. Where?

Domin. Into the dissecting room. When they've *cut her open*, you can go and have a look. (Marius *makes a start toward* Sulla.)

Helena. (*Stopping* Marius) No! No!

Domin. Excuse me, you spoke of lies.

Helena. You wouldn't have her killed?

Domin. *You can't kill machines. Sulla! (Marius one step forward, one arm out. Sulla makes a move toward R. door.)*

Helena. (*Moves a step* R.) Don't be afraid, Sulla. I won't let you go. Tell me, my dear— (*Takes her hand*) —are they always so cruel to you? You mustn't put up with it, Sulla. You mustn't.

Sulla. I am a Robot.

Helena. That doesn't matter. Robots are just as good as we are. Sulla, you wouldn't let yourself be cut to pieces?

Sulla. *Yes. (Hand away.)*

Helena. Oh, you're not afraid of death, then?

Sulla. I cannot tell, Miss Glory.

Helena. Do you know what would happen to you in there?

Sulla. Yes, I should cease to move.

Helena. How dreadful! (*Looks at* Sulla.)

Domin. Marius, tell Miss Glory what you are? (*Turns to* Helena.)

Marius. (*To* Helena) Marius, the Robot.

Domin. Would you take Sulla into the dissecting room?

Marius. (*Turns to* Domin) Yes.

Domin. Would you be sorry for her?

Marius. (*Pause*) I cannot tell.

Domin. What would happen to her?

Marius. She would cease to move. They would put her into the stamping mill.

Domin. That is death, Marius. Aren't you afraid of death?

Marius. No.

Domin. You see, Miss Glory, the Robots have no interest in life. They have no enjoyments. They are *less* than so much grass.

Helena. Oh, stop. Please send them away.

Domin. (*Pushes button*) Marius, Sulla, you may go. (Marius *pivots and exits* R. Sulla *exits* L.)

HELENA. How terrible! (*To* C.) It's outrageous what you are doing. (*He takes her hand.*)

DOMIN. *Why outrageous? (His hand over hers. Laughing.)*

HELENA. I don't know, but it is. Why do you call her "Sulla"?

DOMIN. Isn't it a nice name? (*Hand away.*)

HELENA. It's a man's name. Sulla was a Roman General.

DOMIN. What! Oh! (*Laughs*) We thought that Marius and Sulla were lovers.

HELENA. (*Indignantly*) Marius and Sulla were generals and fought against each other in the year—I've forgotten now.

DOMIN. (*Laughing*) Come here to the window. (*He goes to window* C.)

Helena. WHAT?

DOMIN. Come here. (*She goes.*) Do you see anything? (*Takes her arm. She is on his* R.)

HELENA. Bricklayers.

DOMIN. Robots. All our work people are Robots. And down there, can you see anything?

HELENA. Some sort of office.

DOMIN. A counting house. And in it—

HELENA. A lot of officials.

DOMIN. Robots! All our officials are Robots. And when you see the factory— (*Noon WHISTLE blows. She is scared; puts arm on* DOMIN. *He laughs*) If we don't blow the whistle the Robots won't stop working. In two hours I'll show you the kneading trough. (BOTH *come down stage.* HELENA *is* L.C. *and* DOMIN *is* R.C., *arm in arm.*)

HELENA. Kneading trough?

DOMIN. The pestle for beating up the paste. In each one we mix the ingredients for a thousand Robots at one operation. Then there are the vats for the preparation of liver, brains, and so on. Then you will see the bone factory. After that I'll show you the spinning mill.

HELENA. Spinning mill?

DOMIN. Yes. For weaving nerves and veins. Miles and miles of digestive tubes pass through it at a time.

HELENA. (*Watching his gestures*) Mayn't we talk about something else?

DOMIN. Perhaps it would be better. There's only a *handful* of us among a hundred thousand Robots, and *not one woman.* We talk nothing but the factory *all* day, and *every* day. It's just as if we were under a curse, Miss Glory.

HELENA. I'm *sorry* I said that you were lying. (*A KNOCK at door* R.)

DOMIN. Come in. (*He is* C.)

(From R. enter Dr. Gall, Dr. Fabry, Alquist and Dr. Hallemeier. All act formal—conscious. All click heels as introduced.)

DR. GALL. (*Noisily*) I beg your pardon. I hope we don't intrude.

DOMIN. No, no. Come in. Miss Glory, here are Gall, Fabry, Alquist, Hallemeier. This is President Glory's daughter. (ALL *move to her and shake her hand.*)

HELENA. How do you do?

FABRY. We had no idea—

DR. GALL. Highly honored, I'm sure—

ALQUIST. Welcome, Miss Glory.

BUSMAN. (*Rushes in from* R.) Hello, what's up?

DOMIN. Come in, Busman. This is President Glory's daughter. This is Busman, Miss Glory.

BUSMAN. By Jove, that's fine. (ALL *click heels. He crowds in and shakes her hand*) Miss Glory, may we send a cablegram to the papers about your arrival?

HELENA. No, no, please don't.

DOMIN. Sit down, please, Miss Glory.

(On the line, "Sit down, please," all Six Men try to find her a chair at once. Helena goes for the chair at the extreme L. Domin takes the chair at front of desk, places it in the C. of stage. Hallemeier gets chair at Sulla's typewriter and places it to R. of chair at C. Busman gets armchair from extreme R., but by now Helena has sat in Domin's preferred chair, at C. All sit except Domin. Busman at R. in armchair. Hallemeier R. of Helena. Fabry in swivel chair back of desk.)

BUSMAN. Allow me—

Dr. Gall. PLEASE—

FABRY. Excuse me—

ALQUIST. What sort of a crossing did you have?

Dr. Gall. Are you going to stay long? (Men conscious of their appearance. Alquist's trousers turned up at bottom. He turns them down. Busman polishes shoes. Others fix ties, collars, etc.)

FABRY. What do you think of the factory, Miss Glory?

HALLEMEIER. Did you come over on the *Amelia*?

DOMIN. Be quiet and let *Miss Glory* speak. (MEN *sit erect.* DOMIN *stands at* HELENA'S L.)

HELENA. (*To* DOMIN) What am I to speak to them about? (MEN *look at one another.*)

DOMIN. Anything you like.

HELENA. (*Looks at* DOMIN) May I speak quite frankly?

DOMIN. Why, of course.

HELENA. (*To* OTHERS. *Wavering, then in desperate resolution*) Tell me, doesn't it ever distress you the way you are treated?

FABRY. By whom, may I ask?

HELENA. Why, everybody.

ALQUIST. Treated?

DR. GALL. What makes you think—

HELENA. Don't you feel that you might be living a better life? (*Pause.* ALL *confused.*)

DR. GALL. (*Smiling*) Well, that depends on what you mean, Miss Glory.

HELENA. I mean that it's perfectly outrageous. It's terrible. (*Standing up*) The whole of Europe is talking about the way you're being treated. That's why I came here, to see for myself, and it's a thousand times worse than could have been imagined. How *can* you put *up* with it?

ALQUIST. Put up with what?

HELENA. Good heavens, you are living creatures, just like us, like the whole of Europe, like the whole world. It's disgraceful that you must live like this.

BUSMAN. Good gracious, Miss Glory!

FABRY. Well, she's not far wrong. We live here just like red Indians.

HELENA. Worse than red Indians. May I—oh, may I call you—*brothers*? (MEN *look at each other.*)

BUSMAN. Why not?

HELENA. (*Looking at* DOMIN) Brothers, I have not come here as the President's daughter. I have come on behalf of the Humanity League. Brothers, the Humanity League now has over two hundred thousand members. Two hundred thousand people are on your side, and offer you their help. (*Tapping back of chair.*)

BUSMAN. Two hundred thousand people, Miss Glory; that's a tidy lot. Not bad.

FABRY. I'm always telling you there's nothing like good old Europe. You see they've not forgotten us. They're offering us help.

DR. GALL. What kind of help? A theatre, for instance?

HALLEMEIER. An orchestra?

HELENA. More than that.

ALQUIST. Just you?

HELENA. (*Glaring at* DOMIN) Oh, never mind about me. I'll stay as long as it is necessary. (ALL *express delight.*)

BUSMAN. By Jove, that's good.

ALQUIST. (*Rising* L.) Domin, I'm going to get the best room ready for Miss Glory.

DOMIN. Just a minute. I'm afraid that Miss Glory is of the opinion she has been talking to Robots.

HELEN. Of course. (MEN *laugh*.)

DOMIN. I'm sorry. These gentlemen are human beings just like us.

HELENA. You're not Robots?

BUSMAN. Not Robots.

HALLEMEIER. Robots indeed!

DR. GALL. No, thanks.

FABRY. Upon my honor, Miss Glory, we aren't Robots.

(All together)

HELENA. Then why did you tell me that all your officials are Robots?

DOMIN. Yes, the officials, but not the *managers*. Allow me, Miss Glory— this is Consul Busman, General Business Manager; this is Doctor Fabry, General Technical Manager; Doctor Hallemeier, head of the Institute for the Psychological Training of Robots; Doctor Gall, head of the Psychological and Experimental Department; and Alquist, head of the Building Department, R. U. R. (*As they are introduced they rise and come C. to kiss her hand, except* GALL *and* ALQUIST, *whom* DOMIN *pushes away. General babble.*)

ALQUIST. Just a builder. Please sit down.

HELENA. Excuse me, gentlemen. Have I done something dreadful?

ALQUIST. Not at all, Miss Glory.

BUSMAN. (*Handing flowers*) Allow me, Miss Glory.

HELENA. Thank you.

FABRY. (*Handing candy*) Please, Miss Glory.

DOMIN. Will you have a cigarette, Miss Glory?

HELENA. No, thank you.

DOMIN. Do you mind if I do?

HELENA. Certainly not.

BUSMAN. Well, now, Miss Glory, it is certainly nice to have you with us.

HELENA. (*Seriously*) But you know I've come to disturb your Robots for you. (BUSMAN *pulls chair closer.*)

DOMIN. (*Mocking her serious tone*) My dear Miss Glory— (*Chuckle*) — we've had close upon a hundred saviors and prophets here. Every ship brings us some. Missionaries, Anarchists, Salvation Army, all sorts! It's astonishing what a number of churches and idiots there are in the world.

HELENA. And yet you let them speak to the Robots.

DOMIN. So far we've let them all. Why not? The Robot remembers everything but that's all. They don't even laugh at what the people say. Really it's quite incredible.

HELENA. I'm a stupid girl. Send me back by the first ship.

DR. GALL. Not for anything in the world, Miss Glory. Why should we send you back?

DOMIN. If it would amuse you, Miss Glory, I'll take you down to the Robot warehouse. It holds about three hundred thousand of them.

BUSMAN. Three hundred and forty-seven thousand.

DOMIN. Good, and you can say whatever you like to them. You can read the Bible, recite the multiplication table, whatever you please. You can even preach to them about human rights.

HELENA. Oh, I think that if you were to show them a little love.

FABRY. *Impossible, Miss Glory! Nothing is harder to like than a Robot.*

HELENA. What do you make them for, then?

BUSMAN. Ha, ha, ha! That's good. What are Robots made for?

FABRY. For *work*, Miss Glory. One Robot can replace two and a half *workmen*. The human machine, Miss Glory, was terribly *imperfect*. It had to be removed sooner or later.

BUSMAN. It was too expensive.

FABRY. It was not *effective*. It no longer answers the requirements of *modern engineering*. Nature has no idea of keeping pace with *modern labor*. For example, from a technical point of view, the whole of *childhood* is a sheer absurdity. So much time lost. And then again—

HELENA. (*Turns to* DOMIN) Oh, no, no!

FABRY. Pardon me. What is the real *aim* of your League—the—the Humanity League?

HELENA. Its real purpose is to—to protect the Robots—and—and to insure good treatment for them.

FABRY. Not a bad object, either. A machine has to be treated properly. (*Leans back*) *I don't like damaged articles.* Please, Miss Glory, enroll us all *members* of your league. ("*Yes, yes!*" *from all* MEN.)

HELENA. No, you don't understand me. What we really want is to—to— *liberate* the Robots. (*Looks at all* OTHERS.)

HALLEMEIER. How do you propose to do that?

HELENA. They are to be—to be dealt with like human beings.

HALLEMEIER. Aha! I suppose they're to vote. To drink beer. To order us about?

HELENA. Why shouldn't they drink beer?

HALLEMEIER. Perhaps they're even to receive wages? (*Looking at other* MEN, *amused.*)

HELENA. Of course they are.

HALLEMEIER. Fancy that! Now! And what would they do with their wages, pray?

HELENA. They would buy—what they want—what pleases them.

HALLEMEIER. That would be very nice, Miss Glory, only there's nothing that does please the Robots. Good heavens, what are they to buy? You can feed them on pineapples, straw, whatever you like. It's all the *same* to them. They've no appetite at all. They've no interest in anything. Why, hang it all, nobody's ever yet seen a Robot smile.

HELENA. Why—why don't you make them—happier?

HALLEMEIER. That wouldn't do, Miss Glory. They are only workmen.

HELENA. Oh, but they're so intelligent.

HALLEMEIER. Confoundedly so, but they're nothing else. They've no will of their own. No soul. No passion.

HELENA. No love?

HALLEMEIER. Love? Huh! Rather not. Robots don't love. Not even themselves.

HELENA. No defiance?

HALLEMEIER. Defiance? I don't know. Only *rarely*, from time to time.

HELENA. What happens then?

HALLEMEIER. Nothing particular. Occasionally they seem to go off their *heads*. Something like epilepsy, you know. It's called "Robot's Cramp." They'll suddenly sling down everything they're holding, stand still, gnash their teeth—and then they have to go into the stamping-mill. It's evidently some breakdown in the mechanism.

DOMIN. (*Sitting on desk*) A flaw in the works that has to be removed.

HELENA. No, no, that's the soul.

FABRY. (*Humorously*) Do you think that the soul first shows itself by a gnashing of teeth? (MEN *chuckle*.)

HELENA. Perhaps it's just a sign that there's a struggle within. Perhaps it's a sort of revolt. Oh, if you could infuse them with it.

DOMIN. That'll be remedied, Miss Glory. Doctor Gall is just making some experiments.

DR. GALL. Not with regard to that, Domin. At present I am making *pain* nerves.

HELENA. Pain nerves?

DR. GALL. Yes, the Robots feel practically no bodily pain. You see, young Rossum provided them with too limited a *nervous* system. We *must* introduce *suffering*.

HELENA. Why do you want to cause them pain?

DR. GALL. For industrial reasons, Miss Glory. Sometimes a Robot does damage to himself because it doesn't hurt him. He puts his hand into the machine— (*Describes with gesture*) —breaks his finger— (*Describes with gesture*) —smashes his head. It's all the same to him. We must provide them with *pain*. That's an automatic *protection* against damage.

HELENA. Will they be happier when they feel pain?

DR. GALL. On the contrary; but they will be more perfect from a technical point of view.

HELENA. Why don't you create a soul for them?

DR. GALL. That's not in our power.

FABRY. That's not in our interest.

BUSMAN. That would increase the cost of production. Hang it all, my dear young lady, we turn them out at such a cheap rate—a hundred and fifty dollars each, fully dressed, and fifteen years ago they cost ten thousand. Five years ago we used to buy the *clothes* for them. Today we have our own weaving mill, and now we even *export* cloth five times cheaper than other factories. What do you pay a yard for cloth, Miss Glory?

HELENA. (*Looking at* DOMIN) I don't really know. I've forgotten.

BUSMAN. Good gracious, and you want to found a Humanity League. (MEN *chuckle.*) It only costs a third now, Miss Glory. All prices are today a third of what they were and they'll fall still lower, lower, like that.

HELENA. I don't understand.

BUSMAN. Why, bless you, Miss Glory, it means that the cost of *labor* has fallen. A Robot, food and all, costs three-quarters of a cent per hour. (*Leans forward*) That's mighty important, you know. All factories will go pop like chestnuts if they don't at once buy Robots to lower the cost of production.

HELENA. And get rid of all their workmen?

BUSMAN. Of course. But in the meantime we've dumped five hundred thousand *tropical* Robots down on the Argentine pampas to grow corn. Would you mind telling me how much you pay a pound for bread?

HELENA. I've no idea. (ALL *smile.*)

BUSMAN. Well, I'll tell you. It now costs two cents in good old Europe. A pound of bread for two cents, and the *Humanity League*— (*Designates* HELENA) —knows nothing about it. (*To* MEN) Miss Glory, you don't realize that even *that's* too expensive. (*All* MEN *chuckle.*) Why, in five years' time I'll wager—

Helena. WHAT?

BUSMAN. That the cost of everything will be a tenth of what it is today. Why, in five years we'll be up to our ears in corn and—everything else.

ALQUIST. Yes, and all the workers throughout the world will be unemployed.

DOMIN. (*Seriously. Rises*) Yes, Alquist, they will. Yes, Miss Glory, they will. But in ten years Rossum's Universal Robots will produce so much *corn*, so much *cloth*, so much everything that things will be practically without price.

There will be no poverty. All work will be done by living machines. Everybody will be free from worry and liberated from the degradation of labor. Everybody will live only to *perfect* himself.

Helena. Will he?

Domin. Of course. It's bound to happen. Then the servitude of man to man and the enslavement of man to matter will cease. Nobody will get bread at the cost of life and hatred. The Robots will wash the feet of the beggar and prepare a bed for him in his house.

Alquist. Domin, Domin, what you say sounds too much like Paradise. There was something *good* in *service* and something *great* in humility. There was some kind of virtue in *toil* and *weariness*.

Domin. Perhaps, but we cannot reckon with what is lost when we start out to transform the world. Man shall be *free* and supreme; he shall have no other aim, no other labor, no other care than to perfect himself. He shall serve neither matter nor man. He will not be a machine and a device for production. He will be *Lord* of creation.

Busman. Amen.

Fabry. So be it.

Helena. (*Rises*) You have bewildered me. I should like to believe this.

Dr. Gall. You are younger than we are, Miss Glory. You will live to see it.

Hallemeier. True. (*Looking around*) Don't you think Miss Glory might lunch with us? (*All* Men *rise.*)

Dr. Gall. Of course. Domin, ask her on behalf of us all.

Domin. Miss Glory, will you do us the honor?

Helena. When you know why I've come?

Fabry. For the League of Humanity, Miss Glory.

Helena. Oh, in that case perhaps—

Fabry. That's fine. (*Pause*) Miss Glory, excuse me for five minutes. (*Exits* R.)

Hallemeier. Thank you. (*Exits* R. *with* Dr. Gall.)

Busman. (Whispering) I'll be back soon. (Beckoning to Alquist, they exit.)

Alquist. (*Starts, stops, then to* Helena, *then to door*) I'll be back in exactly five minutes. (*Exits* R.)

Helena. What have they all gone for?

Domin. To cook, Miss Glory. (*On her* L.)

Helena. To cook what?

Domin. Lunch. (*They laugh; takes her hand*) The Robots do our cooking for us and as they've no taste it's not altogether— (*She laughs.*) Hallemeier is awfully *good* at grills and Gall can make any kind of sauce, and Busman knows all about omelets.

Helena. What a feast! And what's the specialty of Mr.—your builder?

Domin. Alquist? Nothing. He only lays the table. And Fabry will get to-gether a little fruit. Our cuisine is very modest, Miss Glory.

Helena. (*Thoughtfully*) I wanted to ask you something—

Domin. And I wanted to ask you something too—they'll be back in five minutes. (*Looks at door* R.)

Helena. What did you want to ask me? (*Sits* C.)

Domin. Excuse me, you asked first. (*Sits* L. *of her.*)

Helena. Perhaps it's silly of me, but why do you manufacture female Robots when—when—

Domin. When sex means nothing to them?

Helena. Yes.

Domin. There's a certain demand for them, you see. Servants, saleswomen, stenographers. People are *used* to it.

Helena. But—but tell me, are the Robots male and female, mutually—completely without—

Domin. Completely indifferent to each other, Miss Glory. There's no sign of any *affection* between them.

Helena. Oh, that's terrible.

Domin. Why?

Helena. It's so unnatural. One doesn't know whether to be disgusted or to hate them, or perhaps—

Domin. To pity them. (*Smiles.*)

Helena. That's more like it. What did you want to ask *me*?

Domin. I should like to ask you, Miss Helena, if you will marry me.

Helena. What? (*Rises.*)

Domin. Will you be my wife? (*Rises.*)

Helena. No. The idea!

Domin. (*To her, looking at his watch*) Another three minutes. If you don't marry me you'll have to marry one of the other five.

Helena. But why should I?

Domin. Because they're *all* going to ask you in turn.

Helena. (*Crossing him to* L.C.) How could they dare do such a thing?

Domin. I'm very sorry, Miss Glory. It seems they've fallen in love with you.

Helena. Please don't let them. I'll—I'll go away at once. (*Starts* R. *He stops her, his arms up.*)

Domin. Helena— (*She backs away to desk. He follows*) You wouldn't be so cruel as to refuse us.

Helena. But, but—I can't marry all six.

Domin. No, but one anyhow. If you don't want *me*, marry Fabry.

Helena. I won't.

Domin. Ah! Doctor Gall?

Helena. I don't want any of you.

Domin. Another two minutes. (Pleading. Looking at watch.)

Helena. I think you'd marry any woman who came here.

Domin. *Plenty* of them have come, Helena.

Helena. (*Laughing*) Young?

Domin. Yes.

Helena. Why didn't you marry one of *them*?

Domin. Because I didn't lose my head. Until today—then as soon as you lifted your veil— (Helena *turns her head away.*) Another minute.

(WARN Curtain.)

Helena. But I don't want you, I tell you.

Domin. (*Laying both hands on her shoulder*) One more minute! Now you either have to look me straight in the eye and say "no" violently, and then I leave you alone—or— (Helena *looks at him. He takes hands away. She takes his hand again.*)

Helena. (Turning her head away) You're mad.

Domin. A man *has* to be a bit mad, Helena. That's the best thing about him. (*He draws her to him.*)

Helena. (*Not meaning it*) You are—you are—

Domin. Well?

Helena. Don't, you're hurting me!

Domin. The last chance, Helena. Now or never—

Helena. But—but— (He embraces her; kisses her. She embraces him. KNOCKING at R. door.)

Domin. (Releasing her) Come in. (She lays her head on his shoulder.)

(Enter Busman, Gall and Hallemeier in kitchen aprons, Fabry with a bouquet and Alquist with a napkin under his arm.)

Domin. Have you finished your job?

Busman. Yes.

Domin. So have we. (He embraces her. The Men rush around them and offer congratulations.)

THE CURTAIN FALLS QUICKLY

ACT TWO

Scene: Helena's drawing room. Ten years later. The skeleton framework of Act I is still used. Tall windows put in back instead of Act I windows. Steel shutters for these windows. Where the green cabinet of Act I at Left has stood is a door, L.2, leading to the outside. Where the cabinet stood at Right, a fireplace is placed. The tall open hallway R.C. of Act I is blocked up with a flat piece. The doors at Right and Left 1 have been changed to those of a drawing room. Door at Right leads to Helena's bedroom. Door at Left 1 leads to library.

The furniture consists of a reading table at Left Center covered with magazines. A chair to the Left of table. In front of table is an armchair covered in chintz. A couch Right Center and back of it is a small table with books and book-ends. On this table a small reading lamp. At Right between doorway and fireplace is a small table. There is a work-basket upon it, with pincushion, needles, etc. Down stage at Right and facing the couch is another armchair used by Alquist. To the Left of fireplace is a straight-backed chair. Upstage at Left near the L.2 door to the outside is a writing desk. There is a lamp upon it, writing paper, etc., a telephone and binoculars.

The walls of the room have been covered with silk to the height of seven feet. This is done in small flats to fit the different spaces and are in place against the permanent set. The two French windows open into the room. At the rise they are open. There is a balcony beyond looking over the harbor. The same telegraph wires and poles from Act I are again visible through the window. The windows are trimmed with gray lace curtains. Binoculars on desk up stage by television.

It is about nine in the morning and SUNLIGHT streams into the room through the open windows. Domin opens the door L.2; tiptoes in. He carries a potted plant. He beckons the Others to follow him, and Hallemeier and Fabry enter, both carrying a potted plant. Domin places flowers on the library table and goes to Right and looks toward Helena's bedroom R.

Hallemeier. *(Putting down his flowers on L.C. table and indicates the door R.) Still asleep?*

Domin. Yes.

HALLEMEIER. Well, as long as she's asleep she can't worry about it. (*He remains at* L.C. *table.*)

DOMIN. She knows nothing about it. (*At* C.)

FABRY. (*Putting plant on writing desk*) I certainly hope nothing happens today.

HALLEMEIER. For goodness sake drop it all. Look, this is a fine cyclamen, isn't it? A new sort, my latest—Cyclamen Helena.

DOMIN. (*Picks up binoculars and goes out into balcony*) No signs of the ship. Things must be pretty bad.

HALLEMEIER. Be quiet. Suppose she heard you.

Domin. (Coming into room, puts glasses on desk) Well, anyway the Ultimus arrived just in time.

FABRY. You really think that today—?

DOMIN. I don't know. (*He crosses to* L.C. *table*) Aren't the flowers fine?

HALLEMEIER. (*Fondles flowers*) These are my primroses. And this is my new jasmine. I've discovered a wonderful way of developing flowers quickly. Splendid varieties, too. Next year I'll be developing marvelous ones.

DOMIN. What next year?

FABRY. I'd give a good deal to know what's happening at Havre with—

HELENA. (*Off* R.) Nana.

DOMIN. Keep quiet. She's awake. Out you go. (ALL *go out on tiptoe through* L.2 *door. Enter* NANA L.1)

Helena. (Calling from R.) Nana?

NANA. Horrid mess! Pack of heathens. If I had *my* say, I'd—

HELENA. (*Backwards in the doorway from* R.) Nana, come and do up my dress.

NANA. I'm coming. So you're up at last. (*Fastening* HELENA's *dress*) My gracious, what brutes!

HELENA. Who? (*Turning.*)

NANA. If you want to turn *around*, then turn around, but I shan't fasten you up.

HELENA. (*Turns back*) What are you grumbling about now?

NANA. These dreadful creatures, these heathens—

Helena. (Turning toward Nana again) The Robots?

NANA. I wouldn't even call them by name.

HELENA. What's happened?

NANA. Another of them here has caught it. He began to smash up the statues and pictures in the drawing room; gnashed his teeth; foamed at the mouth. Worse than an animal.

HELENA. Which of them caught it?

NANA. The one—well, he hasn't got any *Christian* name. The one in charge of the library.

HELENA. Radius?

NANA. That's him. My goodness, I'm scared of them. A spider doesn't scare me as much as them.

HELENA. But Nana, I'm surprised you're not sorry for them.

NANA. Why, you're scared of them too. You know you are. Why else did you bring *me* here?

HELENA. I'm not scared, really I'm not, Nana. I'm only sorry for them.

NANA. You're scared. Nobody could *help* being scared. Why, the dog's scared of them. He won't take a scrap of meat out of their hands. He draws in his tail and howls when he knows they're about.

HELENA. The dog has no sense.

NANA. He's better than *them*, and he knows it. Even the *horse* shies when he meets them. They don't have any young, and a *dog* has young, *everyone* has young—

HELENA. (*Turning back*) Please fasten up my dress, Nana.

NANA. I say it's against God's will to—

HELENA. What is it that smells so nice?

NANA. Flowers.

HELENA. What for?

NANA. Now you can turn around.

HELENA. (*Turns; crosses to* C.) Oh, aren't they lovely? Look, Nana. What's happening today?

NANA. It ought to be the end of the world. (*Enter* DOMIN L.2. *He crosses down front of table* L.C.)

HELENA. (*Crosses to him*) Oh, hello, Harry. (NANA *turns upstage to* L.) Harry, why all these flowers?

Domin. Guess. (This scene is played down in front of L.C. table.)

HELENA. Well, it's not my *birthday*!

DOMIN. Better than that.

HELENA. I don't know. Tell me.

DOMIN. It's ten years ago *today* since you *came* here.

HELENA. Ten years? Today? Why— (*They embrace.*)

Nana. (Muttering) I'm off. (She exits L.1.)

HELENA. Fancy you remembering.

DOMIN. I'm really ashamed, Helena. I didn't.

HELENA. But you—

DOMIN. *They* remembered.

HELENA. WHO?

Domin. Busman, Hallemeier—*all* of them. Put your hand in my pocket.

Helena. (*Takes necklace from his Left jacket pocket*) Oh! Pearls! A necklace! Harry, is this for me?

Domin. It's from Busman.

Helena. But we can't accept it, can we?

Domin. Oh, yes, we can. (*Puts necklace on table* L.C.) Put your hand in the other pocket.

Helena. (Takes a revolver out of his Right pocket) What's that?

Domin. Sorry. Not that. Try again. (*He puts gun in pocket.*)

Helena. Oh, Harry, why do you carry a revolver?

Domin. It got there by mistake.

Helena. You never used to *carry* one.

Domin. No, you're right. (*Indicates breast pocket*) There, that's the pocket.

Helena. (*Takes out cameo*) A cameo. Why, it's a Greek cameo.

Domin. Apparently. Anyhow, Fabry says it is.

Helena. Fabry? Did Mr. Fabry give me that?

Domin. Of course. (*Opens the* L.1 *door*) And look in here. Helena, come and see this. (Both *exit* L.1.)

Helena. (*Off* L.1) Oh, isn't it fine? Is this from you?

Domin. (*Off* L.1) No, from Alquist. And there's another on the piano.

Helena. This must be from you?

Domin. There's a card on it.

Helena. From Doctor Gall. (*Reappearing in* L.1 *doorway*) Oh, Harry, I feel embarrassed at so much kindness.

Domin. (*Enters to up* R. *of table* L.C.) Come here. This is what Hallemeier brought you.

Helena. (*To up* L. *of desk*) These beautiful flowers?

Domin. Yes. It's a new kind. Cyclamen-Helena. He grew them in honor of *you*. They are almost as beautiful as you.

Helena. (*Kissing him*) Harry, why do they all—

Domin. They're awfully fond of you. I'm afraid that my present is a little— Look out of the window. (*Crosses to window and beckons to her.*)

Helena. *Where? (They go out into the balcony.)*

Domin. Into the harbor.

Helena. There's a new ship.

Domin. That's *your* ship.

Helena. Mine? How do you mean?

Domin. (R.) For you to take trips in—for your amusement.

Helena. (L.) Harry, that's a gunboat.

DOMIN. A gunboat? What are you thinking of? It's only a little *bigger* and more *solid* than most ships.

HELENA. Yes, but with guns.

DOMIN. Oh, yes, with a few guns. You'll travel like a *queen*, Helena.

HELENA. What's the meaning of it? Has anything happened?

DOMIN. Good heavens, no. I say, try these pearls. (*Crosses to* R. *of table* L.C.)

HELENA. Harry, have you had bad news?

DOMIN. On the contrary, no letters have arrived for a whole week.

Helena. Nor telegrams? (Coming into the room C.)

DOMIN. Nor telegrams.

HELENA. What does that mean?

DOMIN. *Holidays* for us! We all sit in the office with our feet on the table and take a nap. No letters—no telegrams. Glorious!

HELENA. Then you'll stay with me today?

DOMIN. Certainly. (*Embraces her*) That is, we will see. Do you remember ten years ago today? (*Crosses to* L. *of table* L.C.) Miss Glory, it's a great honor to welcome you. (*They assume the same positions as when they first met ten years before in* DOMIN's *office.*)

HELENA. (*To table*) Oh, Mr. Manager, I'm so interested in your factory. (*She sits* R. *of table.*)

DOMIN. I'm sorry, Miss Glory, it's strictly forbidden. The manufacture of artificial people is a secret.

HELENA. But to oblige the young lady who has come a long way.

DOMIN. (*Leans on table*) Certainly, Miss Glory. I have no secrets from you.

HELENA. *Are you sure, Harry? (Leaning on desk, seriously, his right hand on hers.)*

Domin. Yes. (They gradually draw apart.)

HELENA. But I warn you, sir, this young lady intends to do terrible things.

DOMIN. Good gracious, Miss Glory. Perhaps she doesn't want to marry me.

HELENA. Heaven forbid. She never dreamt of such a thing. But she came here intending to stir up a *revolt* among your *Robots*.

DOMIN. A revolt of the Robots!

HELENA. (*Low voice*) Harry, what's the matter with you?

DOMIN. (*Laughing it off*) A *revolt of the Robots*, that's a fine idea. (*Crosses to back of table. She watches him suspiciously.*) Miss Glory, it would be easier for you to cause bolts and screws to rebel than our Robots. You know, Helena, you're wonderful. You've turned the hearts of us all. (*Sits on table.*)

HELENA. Oh, I was fearfully impressed by you all then. You were all so sure of yourselves, so strong. I seemed like a tiny little girl who had lost her way among—among—

Domin. WHAT?

HELENA. (*Front*) Among huge trees. All my feelings were so *trifling* compared with your *self-confidence*. And in all these years I've never *lost* this anxiety. But you've never felt the *least* misgiving, not even when everything went wrong.

DOMIN. What went wrong?

HELENA. Your plans. You remember, Harry, when the workmen in America revolted against the Robots and smashed them up, and when the people gave the Robots firearms against the rebels. And then when the governments turned the Robots into soldiers, and there were so many *wars*.

DOMIN. (*Getting up and walking about*) We foresaw that, Helena. (*Around table to* R.C.) You see, these are only passing troubles which are bound to happen before the new conditions are *established*. (*Walking up and down, standing at Center.*)

HELENA. You were all so powerful, so overwhelming. The *whole world* bowed down before you. (*Rising*) Oh, Harry! (*Crosses to him.*)

DOMIN. What is it?

HELENA. Close the factory and let's go away. All of us.

DOMIN. I say, what's the meaning of this?

HELENA. I don't know. But can't we go away?

DOMIN. Impossible, Helena! That is, at this particular moment—

HELENA. At once, Harry. I'm so frightened.

DOMIN. (*Takes her*) About what, Helena?

HELENA. It's as if something was falling on top of us, and couldn't be stopped. Oh, take us all away from here. We'll find a place in the world where there's no one else. Alquist will build us a house, and then we'll begin life all over again. (*The TELEPHONE rings.*)

DOMIN. (*Crosses to telephone on desk up* L.) Excuse me. Hello—yes, what? I'll be there at once. Fabry is calling me, my dear. (*Crosses* L.)

Helena. Tell me— (She rushes up to him.)

DOMIN. Yes, when I come back. Don't go out of the house, dear. (*Exits* L.2.)

HELENA. He won't tell me. (NANA *brings in a water carafe from* L.1.) Nana, find me the latest newspapers. Quickly. Look in Mr. Domin's bedroom.

NANA. All right. (*Crosses* R.) He leaves them all over the place. That's how they get crumpled up. (*Continues muttering. Exits* R.)

HELENA. (*Looking through binoculars at the harbor*) That's a warship. U-l-t-i—*Ultimus*. They're loading.

Nana. (*Enters R. with newspapers*) Here they are. See how they're crumpled up.

Helena. (*Crosses down*) *They're old ones. A week old. (Drops papers. Both at front of couch. Nana sits R. of table L.C. Puts on spectacles. Reads the newspapers.) Something's happening, Nana.*

Nana. Very likely. It always does. (*Spelling out the words*) "W-a-r in B-a-l-k-a-n-s." Is that far off?

Helena. Oh, don't read it. It's always the same. Always wars! (*Sits on couch.*)

Nana. What else do you *expect*? Why do you *keep* selling thousands and thousands of these heathens as soldiers?

Helena. I suppose it can't be helped, Nana. We can't know—Domin can't know what they're to be used for. When an order comes for them he must just send them.

Nana. He shouldn't make them. (*Reading from newspaper*) "The Robot soldiers spare no-body in the occ-up-ied terr-it-ory. They have ass-ass-ass-inat-ed ov-er sev-en hundred thous-and cit-iz-ens." Citizens, if you please.

Helena. (*Rises and crosses and takes paper*) It can't be. Let me see. (*Crossing to* Nana) They have assassinated over seven hundred thousand citizens, evidently at the order of their commander. (*Drops paper; crosses up* C.)

Nana. (*Spelling out the words from other paper she has picked up from the floor*) "Re-bell-ion in Ma-drid a-gainst the gov-ern-ment. Rob-ot in-fant-ry fires on the crowd. Nine thou-sand killed and wounded."

Helena. *Oh, stop! (Goes up and looks toward the harbor.)*

Nana. Here's something printed in big letters. "Latest news. At Havre the first org-an-iz-a-tion of Rob-ots has been e-stab-lished. Rob-ots work-men, sail-ors and sold-iers have iss-ued a man-i-fest-o to all Rob-ots through-out the world." I don't understand that. That's got no sense. Oh, good gracious, another murder.

Helena. (*Up* C.) Take those papers away now.

Nana. Wait a bit. Here's something in still bigger type. "Stat-ist-ics of pop-ul-a-tion." What's that?

Helena. (*Coming down to* Nana) Let me see. (*Reads*) "During the past week there has again not been a single birth recorded."

Nana. What's the meaning of that? (*Drops paper.*)

Helena. Nana, no more *people* are being born.

Nana. That's the end, then? (*Removing spectacles*) We're done for.

Helena. Don't talk like that.

Nana. No more people are being born. That's a punishment, that's a punishment.

HELENA. NANA!

NANA. (Standing up) That's the end of the world. (Repeat until off. Picks paper up from floor. She exits L.1.)

HELENA. (Goes up to window) Oh, Mr. Alquist. (ALQUIST off L.2.) Will you come here? Oh, come just as you are. You look very nice in your mason's overalls. (ALQUIST enters L.2, his hands soiled with lime and brick dust. She goes to end of sofa and meets him C.) Dear Mr. Alquist, it was awfully kind of you, that lovely present.

ALQUIST. My hands are soiled. I've been experimenting with that new cement.

HELENA. Never mind. Please sit down. (Sits on couch. He sits on her L.) Mr. Alquist, what's the meaning of Ultimus?

ALQUIST. The last. Why?

HELENA. That's the name of my new ship. Have you seen it? Do you think we're off soon—on a trip?

ALQUIST. Perhaps very soon.

HELENA. All of you with me?

ALQUIST. I should like us all to be there.

HELENA. What is the matter?

ALQUIST. Things are just moving on.

HELENA. Dear Mr. Alquist, I know something dreadful has happened.

ALQUIST. Has your husband told you anything?

HELENA. No. Nobody will tell me anything. But I feel—Is anything the matter?

ALQUIST. Not that we've heard of yet.

HELENA. I feel so nervous. Don't you ever feel nervous?

ALQUIST. Well, I'm an old man, you know. I've got old-fashioned ways. And I'm afraid of all this progress, and these new-fangled ideas.

HELENA. Like Nana?

ALQUIST. Yes, like Nana. Has Nana got a prayer book?

HELENA. Yes, a big thick one.

ALQUIST. And has it got prayers for various occasions? Against thunderstorms? Against illness? But not against progress?

HELENA. I don't think so.

ALQUIST. That's a pity.

HELENA. Why, do you mean you'd like to pray?

ALQUIST. I do pray.

HELENA. How?

ALQUIST. Something like this: "Oh, Lord, I thank thee for having given me toil; enlighten Domin and all those who are astray; destroy their work, and aid mankind to return to their labors; let them not suffer harm in soul or body; deliver us from the Robots, and protect Helena. Amen."

HELENA. (*Touches his arm; pats it*) Mr. Alquist, are you a believer?

ALQUIST. I don't know. I'm not quite sure.

HELENA. And yet you pray?

ALQUIST. That's better than *worrying* about it.

HELENA. And that's enough for you?

ALQUIST. (*Ironically*) It *has* to be.

HELENA. But if you thought you saw the destruction of mankind coming upon us—

ALQUIST. I *do* see it.

HELENA. You mean mankind will be destroyed?

ALQUIST. It's bound to be unless—unless.

Helena. WHAT?

Alquist. Nothing. (Pats her shoulder. Rises) Goodbye. (Exits L.2.)

HELENA. (*Rises. Calling*) Nana, Nana! (NANA *enters* L.1.) Is Radius still there?

NANA. (L.C.) The one who went mad? They haven't come for him yet.

HELENA. Is he still raving?

NANA. No. He's tied up.

HELENA. Please bring him here.

NANA. What?

HELENA. At once, Nana. (*Exits* NANA L.1. HELENA *to telephone*) Hello, Doctor Gall, please. Oh, good day, Doctor. Yes, it's Helena. Thanks for your lovely present. Could you come and see me right away? It's important. Thank you. (*Enter* RADIUS L.1; *looks at* HELENA, *then turns head up* L. *She crosses to him*, L.C.) Poor Radius, you've caught it too? Now they'll send you to the stamping mill. Couldn't you control yourself? Why did it happen? You see, Radius, you are more intelligent than the rest. Doctor Gall took such trouble to make you different. Won't you speak?

RADIUS. (*Looking at her*) Send me to the stamping mill. (*Open and close fists.*)

HELENA. But I don't want them to kill you. What was the trouble, Radius?

RADIUS. (*Two steps toward her. Opens and closes fists*) I won't work for you. Put me into the stamping mill.

HELENA. Do you hate us? Why?

RADIUS. You are not as strong as the Robots. You are not as skillful as the Robots. The Robots can do everything. You only give orders. You do nothing but talk.

HELENA. But someone must give orders.

RADIUS. I don't want a master. I know everything for myself.

Helena. Radius! Doctor Gall gave you a better brain than the rest, better than ours. You are the only one of the Robots that understands perfectly. That's why I had you put into the library, so that you could read everything, understand everything, and then, oh, Radius—I wanted you to show the whole world that the Robots are our equals. That's what I wanted of you.

Radius. I don't want a master. I want to be master over others.

Helena. I'm sure they'd put you in charge of *many* Robots. You would be a *teacher* of the Robots.

Radius. I want to be master over people. (*Head up. Pride.*)

Helena. (*Staggering*) You are mad.

Radius. (*Head down low, crosses toward L.; opens hands*) Then send me to the stamping mill.

Helena. *(Steps to him) Do you think we're afraid of you? (Rushing to desk and writing note.)*

Radius. (*Turns his head uneasily*) What are you going to do? What are you going to do? (*Starts for her.*)

Helena. (*Crosses to* R. *of him*) Radius! (*He cowers. Body sways.*) Give this note to Mr. Domin. (*He faces her.*) It asks them not to send you to the stamping mill. I'm sorry you hate us so.

Dr. Gall. (*Enters* L.2; *goes to* C. *upstage*) You wanted me?

Helena. (*Backs away*) It's about Radius, Doctor. He had an attack this morning. He smashed the statues downstairs.

Dr. Gall. (*Looks at him*) What a pity to *lose* him. (*At* C.)

Helena. Radius isn't going to be put into the stamping mill. (*Stands to the* R. *of* Gall.)

Dr. Gall. But every Robot after he has had an attack—it's a strict order.

Helena. No matter—Radius isn't going, if I can *prevent* it.

Dr. Gall. But I warn you. It's dangerous. Come here to the window, my good fellow. Let's have a look. Please give me a needle or a pin. (*Crosses up* R. Radius *follows.* Helena *gets a needle from work-basket on table* R.)

Helena. What for?

Dr. Gall. *A test. (Helena gives him the needle. Gall crosses up to Radius, who faces him. Sticks it into his hand and Radius gives a violent start.) Gently, gently. (Opens the jacket of Radius and puts his ear to his heart) Radius, you are going into the stamping mill, do you understand? There they'll kill you— (Takes glasses off and cleans them) —and grind you to powder. (Radius opens hands and fingers.) That's terribly painful. It will make you scream aloud. (Opens Radius's eye. Radius trembles.)*

Helena. *Doctor— (Standing near couch.)*

Dr. Gall. No, no, Radius, I was wrong. I forgot that Madame Domin has put in a good word for you, and you'll be left off. (*Listens to heart*) Ah, that *does* make a difference. (Radius *relaxes. Again listens to his heart for a reaction*) All right—you can go.

Radius. You do unnecessary things— (*Exit* Radius L.2.)

Dr. Gall. (*Speaks to her—very concerned*) Reaction of the pupils, increase of sensitiveness. It wasn't an attack characteristic of the Robots.

Helena. What was it, then? (*Sits in couch.*)

Dr. Gall. (C.) Heaven knows. Stubbornness, anger or revolt—I don't know. And his heart, too.

Helena. What?

Dr. Gall. It was fluttering with nervousness like a *human* heart. He was all in a sweat with fear, and—do you know, I don't believe the rascal is a Robot *at all* any longer.

Helena. Doctor, has Radius a soul?

Dr. Gall. (*Over to couch*) He's got something nasty.

Helena. If you knew how he hates us. Oh, Doctor, are all your Robots like that? All the new ones that you began to make in a different way? (*She invites him to sit beside her. He sits.*)

Dr. Gall. Well, some are more sensitive than others. They're all more human beings than Rossum's Robots were.

Helena. Perhaps this hatred is more like human beings, too?

Dr. Gall. That too is *progress*.

Helena. What became of the girl you made, the one who was most like us?

Dr. Gall. Your favorite? I *kept* her. She's lovely, but stupid. No good for work.

Helena. But she's so beautiful.

Dr. Gall. I called her "Helena." I wanted her to resemble *you*. She is a failure.

Helena. In what way?

Dr. Gall. She goes about as if in a dream, remote and listless. She's without life. I watch and wait for a miracle to happen. Sometimes I think to myself: "If you were to wake up only for a moment you would *kill* me for having *made* you."

Helena. And yet you go *on* making Robots! Why are no more children being born?

Dr. Gall. We don't know.

Helena. Oh, but you must. Tell me.

Dr. Gall. You see, so many Robots are being manufactured that people are becoming superfluous. Man is really a survival, but that he should die out, after a paltry thirty years of competition, that's the awful part of it. You might almost think that Nature was *offended* at the manufacture of the Robots, but we still have old Rossum's manuscript.

Helena. Yes. In that strong box.

Dr. Gall. We go on using it and making Robots. All the universities are sending in long petitions to restrict their production. Otherwise, they say, mankind will become extinct through lack of fertility. But the R. U. R. shareholders, of course, won't hear of it. All the governments, on the other hand, are clamoring for an increase in production, to raise the standards of their armies. And all the manufacturers in the world are ordering Robots like mad.

Helena. And has no one demanded that the manufacture should cease altogether?

Dr. Gall. No one has courage.

Helena. Courage!

Dr. Gall. People would stone him to death. You see, after all, it's more convenient to get your work done by the Robots.

Helena. Oh, Doctor, what's going to become of people?

Dr. Gall. God knows. Madame Helena, it looks to us scientists like the end.

Helena. (*She looks out front. Rising*) Thank you for coming and telling me.

Dr. Gall. (*Rises*) That means that you're sending me away.

Helena. Yes. (*Exit* Dr. Gall *L.2. She crosses to* L.C. *To door* L.1. *With sudden resolution*) Nana! Nana! the fire, light it quickly. (Helena *exits* R.)

Nana. (*Entering* L.1) What, light the fire in the summer?

Helena. (*Off* R.) Yes!

Nana. (*She looks for* Radius) Has that mad *Radius* gone?—A fire in summer, what an idea? Nobody would think she'd been *married* ten years. She's like a baby, no sense at all. A fire in summer. Like a baby. (*She lights the fire.*)

Helena. (*Returns from* R. *with armful of faded papers. Back of couch to fireplace, L. of Nana*) Is it burning, Nana? All this has got to be burned.

Nana. What's that?

Helena. Old papers, fearfully old. Nana, shall I burn them?

Nana. Are they any use?

Helena. *No.*

Nana. Well, then, burn them.

Helena. (*Throwing the first sheet on the fire*) What would you say, Nana, if this was money and a lot of money? And if it was an invention, the greatest invention in the world?

NANA. (R. *of fireplace*) I'd say burn it. All these new-fangled things are an offense to the Lord. It's downright wickedness. Wanting to improve the world after He has made it.

HELENA. Look how they curl up. As if they were alive. Oh, Nana, how horrible!

NANA. Here, let me burn them.

HELENA. (*Drawing back*) No, no, I must do it myself. Just look at the flames. They are like hands, like tongues, like living shapes. (*Raking fire with the poker*) Lie down, lie down.

NANA. That's the end of them. (*Fireplace slowly out.*)

HELENA. Nana, Nana!

NANA. Good gracious, what is it you've burned? (*Almost to herself.*)

HELENA. Whatever have I done?

NANA. Well, what is it? (MEN's *laughter off* L.2.)

HELENA. Go quickly. It's the gentlemen calling.

NANA. Good gracious, what a place! (*Exits* L.1.)

DOMIN. (*Opens door* L.2) Come along and offer your congratulations. (*Enter* HALLEMEIER *and* DR. GALL.)

HALLEMEIER. (*Crosses to* R.C.) Madame Helena, I congratulate you on this festive day.

HELENA. Thank you. (*Coming to* C.) Where are Fabry and Busman?

DOMIN. They've gone down the harbor. (*Closes the door and comes to* C.)

HALLEMEIER. Friends, we must *drink* to this happy occasion.

HELENA. (*Crosses* L.) Brandy? With soda water? (*Exits* L.1.)

HALLEMEIER. Let's be temperate. No soda.

DOMIN. What's been burning here? Well, shall I tell her about it?

DR. GALL. (L.C.) Of course. It's all over now.

HALLEMEIER. (*Crosses to* DOMIN. *Embracing* DOMIN) It's all over now. It's all over now. (*They dance around* DR. GALL *in a circle.*) It's all over now.

DOMIN. (*In unison*) It's all over now. (*They keep repeating. Keep it after Helena is on.*)

HELENA. (*Entering* L.1 *with decanter and glasses*) What's all over now? What's the matter with you all? (*She puts tray on* L.C. *table. Dr. Gall helps her to pour the drinks.*)

HALLEMEIER. (*Crosses to back of table*) A piece of good luck. Madame Domin! (ALL *ad lib.*) Just ten years ago today you arrived on this island. (HALLEMEIER *crosses to table for drink.*)

DR. GALL. And now, ten years later to the minute— (*Crosses to* L. *of* HALLEMEIER.)

Hallemeier. *The same ship's returning to us. So here's to luck. (Drinks. Domin with great exuberance has gone out in the balcony and looks over the harbor.)*

Dr. Gall. Madame, your health. (All *drink.*)

Hallemeier. That's fine and strong.

Helena. Which ship did you mean?

Domin. (Crosses down to C. Helena gives him his drink and she crosses to front of couch) Any ship will do, as long as it arrives in time. To the ship. (Empties his glass.)

Helena. You've been waiting for the ship? (*Sits on couch.*)

Hallemeier. Rather. Like Robinson Crusoe. Madame Helena, best wishes. Come along, Domin, out with the news. (Gall *has sat L. of L.C. table, drinking.* Hallemeier *back of table* R.C.)

Helena. Do tell me what's happened?

Domin. First, it's all up. (He puts brandy glass on L.C. table. Hallemeier sits on table, upper end.)

Helena. What's up?

Domin. The revolt.

Helena. What revolt?

Domin. Give me that paper, Hallemeier. (Hallemeier *hands paper.* Domin *reads*) "The first National Robot organization has been founded at Havre, and has issued an appeal to the Robots throughout the world."

Helena. I read that.

Domin. That means a revolution. A revolution of all the Robots in the world.

Hallemeier. By Jove, I'd like to know—

Domin. (C.) Who started it? So would I. There was nobody in the world who could affect the Robots, no agitator, no one, and suddenly this happens, if you please.

Helena. What did they do?

Domin. They got possession of all firearms, telegraphs, radio stations, railways and ships.

Hallemeier. And don't forget that these rascals outnumbered us by at least a thousand to one. A hundredth *part* of them would be enough to *settle* us.

Domin. Remember that this news was brought by the last steamer. That explains the stoppage of all communication, and the arrival of no more ships. We knocked off work a few days ago, and we're just waiting to see when things are to start *afresh.*

Helena. Is that why you gave me a warship? (Gall *fills* Domin's *glass.*)

DOMIN. Oh, no, my dear, I ordered that six months ago. Just to be sure I was on the safe side. But, upon my soul, I was sure then that we'd be on board today.

HELENA. Why six months ago?

DOMIN. Well, there were *signs*, you know. But that's of no consequence. (*Gets glass*) To think that this week the whole of civilization has been at *stake*. Your health, my friends.

HALLEMEIER. Your health, Madame Helena. (ALL *drink to* HELENA.)

HELENA. You say it's all over?

DOMIN. Absolutely.

HELENA. How do you know?

DR. GALL. The boat's coming in. The regular mail boat, exact to the minute by the timetable. It will dock punctually at eleven-thirty.

DOMIN. Punctuality is a fine thing, my friends. That's what keeps the world in order. Here's to punctuality. (MEN *drink.*)

HELENA. Then—everything—is all right?

DOMIN. (*Up* C. *a step*) Practically everything. I believe they've cut the cables and seized the radio station. But it doesn't matter if only the *timetable* holds good. (*Up to window.*)

HALLEMEIER. (*Rises*) If the *timetable* holds good, human laws hold good. Divine laws hold good, the laws of the *universe* hold good, everything holds good that *ought* to hold good. (GALL *applauds.*) The timetable is more significant than the gospel, more than Homer, more than the whole of *Kant*. Madame Helena, the timetable is the most perfect product of the human mind. Madame Helena, I'll fill up my glass. (GALL *hands* HALLEMEIER *the decanter.*)

HELENA. Why didn't you tell me anything about it?

DR. GALL. Heaven forbid.

DOMIN. You mustn't be worried with such things. (*Glass on table* R.C.; *crosses to back of couch.*)

HELENA. But if the revolution had spread as far as here?

DOMIN. You wouldn't know anything about it.

HELENA. WHY?

DOMIN. Because we'd be on board your *Ultimus* and well out at sea. Within a month, Helena, we'd be dictating our own terms to the Robots.

HELENA. I don't understand.

DOMIN. (*Crosses to* C. *toward* GALL *and* HALLEMEIER) We'd take something with us that the Robots could not exist *without*!

HELENA. What, Harry?

Domin. (*Turns to* Hallemeier) The secret of their manufacture. Old Rossum's manuscript. As soon as they found out that they couldn't *make* themselves they'd be on their knees to us.

Dr. Gall. (*Rises*) Madame Domin, that was our trump card. I never had the least fear the Robots would win. How could they against people like us? (*Up to window.* Gall *rises and goes out into the balcony.*)

Helena. *Why didn't you tell me? (She rushes up to the fireplace and sees the ashes.)*

Dr. Gall. Why, the boat's in!

Hallemeier. *Eleven-thirty to the dot. (Rising and going onto the balcony) The good old Amelia that brought Madame Helena to us. (Domin goes out onto the balcony.)*

Dr. Gall. Just ten years ago to the minute.

Hallemeier. They're throwing out the mailbags.

Domin. Busman's waiting for them. And Fabry will bring us the first news. You know, Helena, I'm fearfully curious to know how they— (*Crosses to* C. *She gets away from fire to L. of couch*) —tackled this business in Europe.

Hallemeier. (*Crosses down to table*) To think we weren't in it, we who invented the Robots! (*Returning to the armchair.*)

Helena. *Harry— (Rushing to Domin from fireplace.)*

Domin. What is it?

Helena. Let's leave here.

Domin. Now, Helena? Oh, come, come.

Helena. As quickly as possible, all of us!

Domin. Why?

Helena. Please, Harry. Please, Doctor Gall, Hallemeier, please close the factory.

Domin. Why, none of us could leave here now.

Helena. Why?

Domin. Because we're about to *extend* the manufacture of the Robots.

Helena. What, now, now after the revolt?

Domin. Yes, precisely, after the revolt. We're just beginning the manufacture of a new kind.

Helena. What kind?

Domin. Henceforward we shan't have just one factory. There won't be *Universal* Robots any more. We'll establish a factory in every country, in every state, and do you know what these new factories will make?

Helena. No, what?

Domin. *National* Robots.

Helena. How do you mean?

Domin. I mean that each of these factories will produce Robots of a different color, a different language. They'll be complete strangers to each other. (*Turns; takes in* Hallemeier *and* Gall) They'll never be able to understand each other. Then we'll egg them on a little in the matter of misunderstanding and the result will be that for ages to come every Robot will hate every other Robot of a different factory mark. *So humanity will be safe.*

Hallemeier. (*To each of them*) By Jove, we'll make Negro Robots and Swedish Robots and Czechoslovakian Robots, and then—

Helena. Harry, that's dreadful.

Hallemeier. Madame Domin, here's to the hundred new factories. The *National* Robots. (Gall *back of table* L.C.)

Domin. Helena, mankind can only keep things going for another hundred years at the outside. For a hundred years man *must* be allowed to develop and achieve the most he can.

Helena. Oh, *close* the factory before it's too late.

Domin. I tell you we are just beginning on a bigger scale than ever. (*Enter* Fabry L.2; *goes to* L. *of* Domin.)

Dr. Gall. Well, Fabry?

Domin. What's happened? Have you been down to the boat?

Dr. Gall. Let's hear.

Fabry. Read that, Domin. (He hands him a pink handbill. When Domin receives the handbill he sees at once that something has happened.)

Hallemeier. Tell us, Fabry.

Fabry. (*Falsely*) Well, everything is all right—comparatively. (*To the other* Men) On the whole, much as we expected.

Dr. Gall. They acquitted themselves splendidly.

Fabry. Who?

Dr. Gall. The *people.*

Fabry. (*Hesitating*) Oh, yes, of course. That is—Excuse me, there is something we ought to discuss alone.

Helena. (*Touches his arm*) Fabry, have you had bad news?

Fabry. No, no, on the contrary. I only think that we better go into the office.

Helena. Stay here. I'll go. (*Exits* L.1.)

Dr. Gall. What's happened?

Domin. Damnation! (*Coming down to* R.C.)

Fabry. Bear in mind that the *Amelia* brought whole bales of these leaflets. No other cargo at all. (Gall *closes the door* L.2.)

Hallemeier. What? But it arrived on the minute.

Fabry. The Robots are great on punctuality. *Read it*, Domin.

Domin. (R.C. *Reads handbill*) "Robots throughout the world. We, the first International organization of Rossum's Universal Robots, proclaim man our enemy, and an outlaw in the universe." Good heavens, who *taught* them these phrases?

Dr. Gall. Go on.

Domin. They say they are more highly developed than man; stronger and more intelligent. The man's their parasite. Why, it's absurd.

Fabry. Read the third paragraph.

Domin. "Robots throughout the world, we command you to kill all mankind. Spare no man. Spare no woman. Save factories, railways, machinery, mines and raw materials. Destroy the rest. Then return to work. Work must not be stopped." (*Looks at* Others.)

Dr. Gall. That's ghastly.

Hallemeier. The devil!

Domin. "These orders are to be carried out as soon as received." Then come the detailed instructions. Is this actually being *done*, Fabry?

Fabry. Evidently. (Busman *rushes in* L.2 *and collapses on couch* R.C.) By Jove, that was a sprint!

Busman. Well, boys, I suppose you've heard the glad news.

Domin. Quick on board the *Ultimus*.

Busman. Wait, Harry, wait. There's no hurry.

Domin. Why wait?

Busman. Because it's no good, my boy. The Robots are already on board the *Ultimus*.

Dr. Gall. That's ugly.

Domin. Fabry, telephone the electrical works. (Fabry *goes to back of couch*.)

Busman. No use, my boy. They've charged the air with static.

Domin. (Inspects his revolver) Well, then, I'll go. (Starts L.; stops.)

Busman. Where?

Domin. To the electrical works. There are some *people* still there. I'll bring them across. (*Gets as far as* L.2 *door*.)

(*WARN Curtain.*)

Busman. Better not try it.

Domin. Why?

Busman. Because I'm very much afraid we are surrounded. (All *rush out into the balcony*.)

Dr. Gall. Surrounded? (*Runs to window*) I rather think you're right. (Gall *rushes to balcony*.)

Hallemeier. By Jove, that's deuced quick work. (*Going to windows*.)

HELENA. (*Runs in L.1. To L.*) Harry, what's this? (*Holds out paper.*)

DOMIN. Where did you get it? (*Coming to C.*)

Helena. (Points to the manifesto of the Robots which she has in her hand) The Robots in the kitchen!

DOMIN. Where are the ones that brought it?

HELENA. There, gathered around the house. (GALL, HALLEMEIER, DOMIN *start down* C.)

(*The factory WHISTLE blows. Mob VOICES start.*)

DOMIN. The factory whistle! (FABRY, GALL, HALLEMEIER *looking over* C.; *then turn* R.)

Busman. NOON?

DOMIN. (*Looking at his watch. To* HALLEMEIER) No! That's not noon yet. That must be—that's— (*Front.*)

HELENA. WHAT?

DOMIN. The Robots' signal—the attack!

(*Helena clings to Domin. Fabry and Gall close the steel shutters on window C. Busman hurries to window and looks through the shutters. The Curtain falls quickly with Helena in Domin's arms. The WHISTLE blows until the Curtain is down.*)

CURTAIN

ACT THREE

Scene: *Helena's drawing-room as before. The room is dark and gray. The steel shutters which are outside are still closed as at the end of Act II. Alquist is sitting in chair down stage at extreme R. Domin comes into the room, L.2. (Subdued voices.) Dr. Gall is looking out of the window at Center. He is seated in a chair.*

DOMIN. (*Gets binoculars from desk; crosses up to window. To Gall*) Any more of them?

DR. GALL. Yes. There standing like a wall, beyond the garden railing. Why are they so quiet? It's monstrous to be besieged with silence.

DOMIN. (*Looking through the barred windows*) I should like to know what they are waiting for? They must make a start any minute now. If they lean against the railings it will snap like a match.

DR. GALL. They aren't armed.

DOMIN. (*Puzzled*) We couldn't hold our own for five minutes. Man alive, they overwhelm us like an avalanche. Why don't they make a rush for it? I say. (*Turns to* GALL.)

Dr. Gall. WELL?

DOMIN. I'd like to know what will become of us in the next ten minutes. They've got us in a vise. We're done for, Gall.

DR. GALL. You know, we made one serious mistake.

Domin. WHAT?

DR. GALL. We made the Robots' faces too much alike. A hundred thousand faces all alike, all facing this way. A hundred thousand expressionless bubbles. It's like a nightmare.

DOMIN. You think if they'd been different—

DR. GALL. It wouldn't have been such an awful sight!

DOMIN. (*Looks through binoculars towards the harbor*) I'd like to know what they're unloading from the *Amelia*.

DR. GALL. Not firearms.

FABRY. (*Enters L.2 with a plug-box to which is attached a long cable or wire. Hallemeier following him. Fabry attaches the cable to an electric installation which is on the floor near the wall, down stage at L.1 entrance) All right, Hallemeier, lay down that wire.*

HALLEMEIER. (*Just inside the room*) That was a bit of work. What's the news? (*Seeing* DOMIN *and* GALL *at the window.*)

DR. GALL. We're completely surrounded.

HALLEMEIER. (*Crosses to window*) We've barricaded the passages and the stairs. (*Going to window*) God, what swarms of them. I don't like the looks of them, Domin. There's a feeling of death about it all. Any water here?

FABRY. Ready!

DR. GALL. (*Turning round in the chair*) What's that wire for, Fabry?

FABRY. The electrical installation. Now we can run the current all along the garden railing. (*Up to window*) Whenever we like. If anyone touches it he'll know it. We've still got some *people* there anyhow.

Dr. Gall. WHERE?

FABRY. In the electrical works. At least, I hope so. (*Goes to lamp on table L.C. and turns on lamp*) Ah, they're there, and they're working. As long as that'll burn we're all right. (*To window.*)

HALLEMEIER. The barricades are *all right*, too, Fabry.

FABRY. *Your* barricades! I can put twelve hundred volts into that railing. (HELENA *is playing Rachmaninoff's Elegie off* L.1.)

DOMIN. *Where's Busman?* (*Domin has left window and is walking up and down stage across front.*)

FABRY. Downstairs in the office. He's working out some calculations.

DOMIN. I've called him. We must have a conference. (*Crosses to* L.)

ALQUIST. *Thank God Madame Helena can still play.* (*Hallemeier crosses to L.1 door, opens it slightly and listens to music. Enter Busman L.2.*)

FABRY. Look out, Bus—look out for the wires.

DR. GALL. What's that you're carrying?

BUSMAN. (*Laying the books on the table* L.C.) The ledger, my boy. I'd like to wind up the accounts before—before— (DOMIN *crosses up to window.*) Well, this time I shan't wait till the New Year to strike a balance. What's up? (*Goes to window*) Absolutely quiet.

DR. GALL. Can't you see anything?

BUSMAN. Nothing but blue—blue everywhere.

DR. GALL. That's the Robots.

DOMIN. The Robots are unloading *firearms* from the *Amelia.*

BUSMAN. *Well, what of it? How can I stop them?* (*Returns to* L.C. *table, sits and opens ledger.*)

DOMIN. We can't stop them.

BUSMAN. Then let me go on with my accounts. (*Goes on with his work.*)

Domin. (*Picks up telescope*) Good God! The *Ultimus* has trained her guns on us.

Dr. Gall. Who's *done that*?

Domin. The Robots on board.

Fabry. H'm, then of course— (*Pause*) Then—then that's the end of us. (*To R. corner of desk.*)

Dr. Gall. You mean?

Fabry. The Robots are practised marksmen.

Domin. Yes. It's inevitable. (*Pause.*)

Dr. Gall. (*Swinging around; looking into room. Pause*) That was criminal of old Europe to teach the Robots to fight. Damn them. Couldn't they have given us a rest with their politics? It was a crime to make soldiers of them.

Alquist. It was a crime to make Robots.

Domin. (*Quietly. Down* C.) No, Alquist, I don't regret that even today.

Alquist. Not even today?

Domin. (*Dreamily*) Not even today, the last day of civilization. It was a colossal achievement.

Busman. (*Sotto voce*) Three hundred sixty million.

Domin. (*From window*) Alquist, this is our last hour. We are already speaking half in the other world. That was not an evil *dream* to shatter the servitude of labor. The dreadful and humiliating *labor* that man had to undergo. Work was too hard. *Life* was too hard. And to overcome that—

Alquist. Was not what the two Rossums dreamed of. Old Rossum only thought of his Godless tricks, and the young one of his milliards. And that's not what your R. U. R. *shareholders* dream of either. They dream of dividends, and their dividends are the ruin of mankind.

Domin. To Hell with your dividends. (*Crossing* R. *in front of couch*) Do you suppose I'd have done an hour's work for them? It was for myself that I worked, for my own satisfaction. I wanted man to become the master. So that he *shouldn't* live merely for the crust of bread. I wanted not a single soul to be broken by other people's machinery. I wanted nothing, nothing, nothing to be left of this appalling social structure. I'm revolted by poverty. I wanted a new generation. I wanted—I thought—

Alquist. Well?

Domin. (*Front of couch*) I wanted to turn the whole of mankind into an aristocracy of the world. An aristocracy nourished by millions of mechanical slaves. Unrestricted, free and consummated in man. And maybe more than man.

Alquist. Superman?

Domin. Yes. Oh, only to have a hundred years of time. Another hundred years for the future of mankind.

Busman. (*Sotto voce*) Carried forward—four hundred and twenty millions. (Domin *sits on couch.*)

Hallemeier. (*Pauses—back of couch*) What a fine thing music is. We ought to have gone in for that before.

Fabry. Gone in for what?

Hallemeier. Beauty, lovely things. What a lot of lovely things there are. The world was wonderful, and we—we here—tell me, what enjoyment did we *have*?

Busman. (*Sotto voce*) Five hundred and twenty million.

Hallemeier. Life was a good thing, life was— (*Looking out of window. Directly to* Fabry) Fabry, switch the current into that railing.

Fabry. *Why? (Rushes to electric installation at L.)*

Hallemeier. They're grabbing hold of it. (Domin *rises—straightens up.* All *rise.*)

Dr. Gall. Connect it up.

Hallemeier. Fine, that's doubled them up. Two, three, four killed.

Dr. Gall. They're retreating. (Domin *sits.*)

Hallemeier. Five killed.

Dr. Gall (*Pause*) The first encounter.

Hallemeier. They're charred to cinders, my boy. Who says we must give in? (*MUSIC stops.*)

Domin. (Alquist *and* Gall *sit. Wiping his forehead*) Perhaps we've been killed this hundred years and are only ghosts. It's as if I had been through all this before, as if I'd already had a mortal wound here in the throat. (*Looking at each as he speaks*) And you, Fabry, had once been shot in the head. And you, Gall, torn limb from limb. And Hallemeier knifed.

Hallemeier. Fancy me being knifed. (*Looks at each. Then speaks*) Why are you so quiet, you fools? (*Steps down*) Speak, can't you?

Alquist. And who is to blame for all this?

Hallemeier. Nobody is to blame except the Robots.

Alquist. No, it is *we* are to blame. You, Domin, myself—all of us. For our own selfish ends, for profit, for progress, we have destroyed mankind. Now we'll *burst* with all our greatness.

Hallemeier. Rubbish, man. Mankind can't be wiped out so easily.

Alquist. It's our fault. It's our fault. (*Rises, coming* R. *of* Gall.)

Dr. Gall. No! I'm to blame for this, for everything that's happened. (*He leaves the window and comes down to end of couch.*)

Fabry. You, Gall?

Dr. Gall. I changed the Robots.

Busman. What's that?

Dr. Gall. I changed the character of the Robots. I changed the way of making them. Just a few details about their bodies. Chiefly—chiefly, their—their irritability.

Hallemeier. Damn it, why?

Busman. What did you do it for?

Fabry. Why didn't you say anything?

Dr. Gall. I did it in secret. I was transforming them into human beings. In certain respects they're already *above* us. They're stronger than we are.

Fabry. And what's that got to do with the revolt of the Robots?

Dr. Gall. Everything, in my opinion. They've ceased to be machines. They're already *aware* of their *superiority*, and they hate us as they hate everything human.

Domin. Perhaps we're only phantoms.

Fabry. Stop, Harry. We haven't much time, Doctor Gall.

Domin. Fabry, Fabry, how your forehead bleeds where the shot pierced it.

Fabry. (*Crosses to* Gall) Be silent! Doctor Gall, you admit changing the way of making the Robots.

Dr. Gall. Yes.

Fabry. Were you aware of what might be the consequences of your experiment?

Dr. Gall. I was bound to reckon with such a possibility.

Fabry. (*Amusing*) Why did you do it, then?

(Helena enters L.1.)

Dr. Gall. For my own satisfaction. The experiment was my own.

Helena. That's not true, Doctor Gall! (*Crosses to couch.*)

Domin. (*Rises*) Helena, you? (*Crosses to her*) Let's look at you. Oh, it's terrible to be dead. (*He rises and crushes her in his arms.*)

Helena. Stop, Harry.

Domin. No, no, Helena, don't leave me now. You are *life* itself.

Helena. No, dear, I won't leave you. But I must tell them. Doctor Gall is not guilty.

Fabry. Excuse me. Gall was under certain obligations.

Helena. No. He did it because I wanted it. Tell them, Doctor Gall—how many years ago did I ask you to—?

Dr. Gall. I did it on my own responsibility.

Helena. Don't believe him. I asked him to give the Robots souls.

Domin. This has nothing to do with the soul.

Helena. That's what he said. He said that he could change only a physiological—a physiological—

Hallemeier. (*From up at window*) A physiological correlate?

Helena. Yes. But it meant so much to me that he should do even that.

Domin. Why?

Helena. I thought that if they were more like us they would understand us better. That they couldn't hate us if they were only a little more human.

Domin. Nobody can hate man more than man.

Helena. Oh, don't speak like that, Harry. It was so terrible, this cruel strangeness between us and them. That's why I asked Gall to *change* the Robots. I swear to you that he didn't want to.

Domin. But he did it.

Helena. Because I asked him.

Dr. Gall. I did it for myself as an experiment. (*Up to window.*)

Helena. No, Doctor Gall! I know you wouldn't refuse me.

Domin. Why?

Helena. You know, Harry.

Domin. Yes, because he's in *love* with you—like all of them. (Fabry *up to window. Pause.* Domin *takes her in his arms.*)

Hallemeier. Good God, they're sprouting up out of the earth. Why, perhaps these very walls will change into Robots.

Busman. (*Rises; crosses to* Gall) Gall, when did you actually start these tricks of yours?

Dr. Gall. Three years ago.

Busman. Aha. And on how many Robots altogether did you *carry out* your improvements? (*Walking to and fro.*)

Dr. Gall. A few hundred of them.

Busman. Ah! That means for every million of the good old Robots there's only one of Gall's improved pattern. (*Back to table* L.C.)

Domin. *What of it? (Crossing around L., he stands upstage in the L.2 doorway.)*

Busman. That it's of no consequence whatsoever.

Fabry. Busman's right. (Helena *sits in armchair* R. *of* L.C. *table.*)

Busman. I should think so, my boy; but do you know what is to blame for this lovely mess?

Fabry. What?

Busman. The number! (*Crosses to* L. *of* L.C. *table*) Upon my soul, we might have known that some day or other the Robots would be stronger than human beings, and that this was bound to happen. And we were doing all we could to bring it about as soon as possible. You, Domin, you, Fabry, myself—

Domin. Are you accusing us? (*Turning on him.*)

Busman. Oh, do you suppose the management controls the output? It's the demand that controls the output.

Helena. And is it for that we must perish?

Busman. That's a nasty word, Madame Helena. We don't want to perish. I don't, anyhow. (*He sits* L. *of table.*)

Domin. No? What do you want to do?

Busman. I want to get out of this, that's all.

Domin. Oh, stop it, Busman.

Busman. Seriously, Harry, I think we might try it.

Domin. *How? (To front again.)*

Busman. By fair means. I do everything by fair means. Give me a free hand and I'll *negotiate* with the Robots.

Domin. By fair means?

Busman. (*Rises*) Of course. For instance, I'll say to them: "Worthy and Worshipful Robots, you have everything. You have intellect, you have power, you have *firearms*. But we have just one interesting screed, a dirty old yellow scrap of paper—"

Domin. *Rossum's manuscript? (Interest from All. Gall is at C., near couch. Hallemeier is up at window C.)*

Busman. Yes. "And that," I'll tell them, "contains an account of your illustrious origin, the noble process of your manufacture and so on. Worthy Robots, without this scribble on that paper you will not be able to produce a single new colleague. In another twenty years there will not be the living specimen of a Robot whom you could exhibit in a menagerie. My esteemed friends, that would be a great *blow* to you, *but* if you will let all of us human beings on Rossum's Island go on board that ship we will *deliver* the factory and the secret of the process to you in return. *You* allow *us* to get away, and *we* will allow *you* to *manufacture* yourselves. That, worthy Robots, is a fair deal. Something for something." That's what I'd say to them, my boys. (*Sits.*)

Domin. (*Crosses to* C.) Busman, do you think we'd sell the manuscript?

Busman. Yes, I do. If not in a friendly way, then—either we sell it or they'll find it. Just as you like.

Domin. Busman, we can *destroy* Rossum's manuscript.

Busman. Then we destroy everything—not only the manuscript but ourselves. Just as you think fit.

Domin. There are over thirty of us on this island. Are we to sell the secret? And save that many souls at the risk of enslaving mankind—

Busman. Why, you're mad. Who'd sell the *whole* manuscript?

Domin. Busman, no cheating! (*To* L.C. *table.*)

Busman. Well then, sell, but afterwards—

Domin. Well?

BUSMAN. Let's suppose this happens. When we're on board the *Ultimus* I'll stop up my ears with cotton wool, lie down somewhere in the hold, and you'll train the guns on the factory and blow it to smithereens, and *with* it Rossum's secret.

FABRY. (*Rises*) No!

DOMIN. Busman, you're no—gentleman. If we sell them it will be a straight sale.

BUSMAN. (*Rises*) It's in the interest of humanity to—

DOMIN. It's in the interest of humanity to keep our word—

HALLEMEIER. Oh, come, what rubbish!

DOMIN. This is a fearful decision. We are selling the destiny of mankind. Are we to sell or destroy? Fabry?

FABRY. SELL.

Domin. GALL?

Dr. Gall. SELL.

DOMIN. Hallemeier?

HALLEMEIER. Sell, of course.

DOMIN. Alquist?

ALQUIST. As God wills.

DOMIN. (*Starts off* R.) Very well, gentlemen.

HELENA. Harry, you're not asking *me*.

DOMIN. (*Stops. To her*) No, child. (*Starting* R.) Don't you worry about it. (*He pats her shoulder.*)

FABRY. Who'll do the negotiating?

Busman. I will. (Up to window.)

DOMIN. Wait till I bring the manuscript. (DOMIN *goes out* R.)

HELENA. *(Rises) Harry, don't go! (Helena sits. All look at her. Pause.)*

FABRY. (*Looking out of window*) Oh, to escape you! you—*matter*—in revolt; oh, to preserve human life, if only upon a *single* vessel—

DR. GALL. Don't be afraid. (*Going to back of couch*) Madame Helena. We'll sail far away from here; we'll begin life all over again.

HELENA. Oh, Gall, don't speak.

FABRY. (*Crosses to* L. *of* GALL) It isn't too late. (*Going to* L. *of her chair*) It will be a little State with one ship. Alquist will build us a house and you shall rule over us.

HALLEMEIER. (*Crosses to* L. *of* FABRY) Madame Helena, Fabry's right.

HELENA. (*Breaking down*) Oh, stop! Stop!

BUSMAN. Good! (*Crosses to* L. *of* L.C. *table*) I don't mind beginning all over again. That suits me right down to the ground. (*Going through papers on table.*)

Fabry. And this little State of ours could be the center of future life. A place of refuge where we could gather strength. Why, in a few hundred years we could conquer the world again.

Alquist. You believe that even today?

Fabry. Yes!

Busman. *Amen.* You see, Madame Helena, we're not so badly off.

Domin. (*Storms into* R. *To* R. *of couch. Hoarsely*) Where's old Rossum's manuscript? (*To* R.C.)

Busman. In your strong-box, of course.

Domin. Someone—has—stolen it!

Dr. Gall. Impossible.

Domin. Who has stolen it?

Helena. (*Standing up*) I did. (*Reactions from Fabry and Hallemeier.*)

Domin. Where did you put it?

Helena. Harry, I'll tell you everything. Only forgive me.

Domin. Where did you put it?

Helena. (*Pointing to fireplace*) This morning—I burnt—the two copies.

Domin. Burnt them? Where—in the fireplace? (*Goes to fireplace, followed by* Fabry, Hallemeier *and* Busman.)

Helena. (*Throwing herself on her knees. By sofa, facing upstage*) For Heaven's sake, Harry.

Domin. (*Going to fireplace*) Nothing—nothing but ashes. Wait, what's this? (*Picks out a charred piece of paper and reads, "By adding." Fabry, Gall and Hallemeier move up to him.*)

Dr. Gall. Let's see. "By adding biogen to—" That's all.

Domin. Is that part of it?

Dr. Gall. (*Carrying paper down and letting it fall*) Yes. (*Gall crosses to L.C. Hallemeier to R. of L.C. table; Fabry to window; Busman to L. of L.C. table.*)

Busman. God in Heaven! (*Sits L. of table.*)

Domin. Then we're done for. Get up, Helena.

Helena. Then you've forgiven me?

Domin. Get up, child. I can't bear—

Fabry. (*Lifting her up*) Please don't torture us.

Helena. Harry, what have I done?

Fabry. (*Coming to* Helena) Don't, Madame Helena.

Domin. (*Takes* Helena *to couch. She sits.*) Gall, you couldn't draw up Rossum's formula from memory?

Dr. Gall. It's out of the question. Even with my recent experiments, I couldn't work without referring to the formula— (*At* L.C.) It's extremely complicated.

Domin. Try. All our lives depend upon it.

Dr. Gall. Without experiments it's impossible.

Domin. And with experiments?

Dr. Gall. It might take years. Besides, I'm not old Rossum.

Busman. God in Heaven! God in Heaven!

Domin. (*Up to fireplace*) So then this was the greatest triumph of the human intellect. These ashes.

Helena. Harry, what have I done?

Domin. (*Comes to her*) Why did you burn it?

Helena. I have destroyed you.

Busman. God in Heaven!

Domin. (*Sits* R. *of her*) Helena, why did you do it, dear?

Helena. I wanted all of us to go away. I wanted to put an end to the factory and everything. It was so awful.

Domin. What was awful?

Helena. That children had stopped being born. Because human beings were not needed to do the work of the world. That's why—

Domin. Is that what you were thinking of? Well, perhaps in your own way you are right.

Busman. Wait a bit. (*Rising*) Good God, what a fool I am not to have thought of it before.

Hallemeier. WHAT?

Busman. Five hundred and twenty millions in bank-notes and checks. Half a billion in our safe. *They'll* sell for *half* a billion—for half a billion they'll— (*Crosses to* Domin.)

Dr. Gall. Are you mad, Busman?

Busman. I may not be a gentleman, but for a half a billion— (*Crosses back to* L.)

Domin. Where are you going? (Gall *clutches* Busman.)

Busman. Leave me alone. Leave me alone! Good God, for half a billion anything can be bought. (Gall *and* Hallemeier *after him, then stop. He rushes out* L.2. Fabry, Gall *and* Hallemeier *to window.*)

Fabry. They stand there as if turned to stone—waiting as if something dreadful could be wrought by their silence—

Hallemeier. (*Looking out window*) The spirit of the mob.

Fabry. Yes. It hovers above them like a quivering of the air.

Helena. Oh, God! Doctor Gall, this is ghastly!

Fabry. There is nothing more terrible than the mob. The one in front is their leader. (Domin *crosses to window.*)

Helena. *(Rises)* Which one? *(Rushing to window.)*

HALLEMEIER. Point him out.

FABRY. (L. *window*) The one at the edge of the dock. This morning I saw him talking to the sailors in the harbor.

Helena. Doctor Gall, that's Radius. (Backing into the room, horror-stricken.)

DR. GALL. YES.

DOMIN. Radius! Radius!

HALLEMEIER. Could you get him from here, Fabry?

FABRY. I hope so.

HALLEMEIER. Try it, then.

FABRY. *Good— (Draws his revolver and takes his aim.)*

HELENA (*To* FABRY) Fabry, don't shoot him.

FABRY. He's their leader.

DR. GALL. *Fire! (Standing above table L.C.)*

HELENA. *Fabry, I beg of you. (She goes to Fabry and holds his arm.)*

FABRY. *(Pause. Lowering the revolver) Very well.*

DOMIN. It was Radius' life I spared.

DR. GALL. Do you think that a Robot can be grateful? (*Pause.*)

FABRY. Busman's going out to them.

HALLEMEIER. He's carrying something. Papers. That's money. Bundles of money. What's that for?

DOMIN. Surely he doesn't want to sell his life. (*He rushes to window* C.) Busman, have you gone mad?

FABRY. He's running up to the railing. Busman. Busman.

HALLEMEIER. (*Yelling*) Busman, come back.

FABRY. He's talking to the Robots. He's showing them the money.

HALLEMEIER. He's pointing to us.

HELENA. He wants to buy us off.

FABRY. He'd better not touch the *railing*.

HALLEMEIER. Now he's waving his arms about.

DOMIN. Busman, come back!

FABRY. Busman, keep away from that railing. Don't touch it, damn you. Quick, switch off the current. (DOMIN *runs to* L. HELENA *screams and* ALL *drop back from the window.*) The current has killed him.

ALQUIST. *(Pause) The first one. (Still in chair down R. Helena sits in chair at window.)*

FABRY. Dead, with half a *billion* by his side. (*Crosses down to table L.C.*)

HALLEMEIER. All honor to him. He wanted to buy us life. (*Crosses to chair* L. *Pause. WIND machine begin.*)

DR. GALL. Do you hear?

DOMIN. A roaring. Like a wind. (*To* L.)

Dr. Gall. Like a storm.

Fabry. (*Lighting the table lamp at table* L.C.) The dynamo is still going—our people are still *there*.

Hallemeier. It was a great thing to be a man. (*Facing lamp from up* C.) There was something *immense* about it.

Fabry. (*Facing the lamp*) From man's thought and man's power came this light, our last hope. (*Leaning over lamp.*)

Hallemeier. (*Facing lamp*) Man's power! May it keep watch over us. (*Leaning over lamp.*)

Alquist. (*Facing lamp*) Man's power.

Domin. (*At corner of table down* L.C. *Facing lamp*) Yes! A torch to be given from hand to hand from age to age forever! (*The LAMP goes out. EXPLOSIONS.*)

Hallemeier. *The end.*

Fabry. *The electric works have fallen! (Terrific EXPLOSIONS outside. More EXPLOSIONS.)*

Domin. In here, Helena. (*He takes* Helena *off through door* R. *and re-enters*) Now quickly! Who'll be on the lower doorway?

Dr. Gall. I will. (*Rushes out* L.2.)

Domin. (*Near couch*) Who on the stairs?

Fabry. I will. You go with her. (*Going out* L.2.)

Domin. The ante room?

Alquist. I will. (He rises and goes toward the L.1.)

Domin. Have you got a revolver?

Alquist. Yes, but I won't shoot.

Domin. What will you do, then?

Alquist. (*Going out* L.1) Die.

Hallemeier. *I'll stay here. (EXPLOSIONS. Rapid firing of MACHINE GUN from below.) Go to her, Harry.*

Domin. *Yes, in a second. (Gets from fireplace and examines two Browning guns.)*
(WARN Curtain.)

Hallemeier. Confound it, go to her.

Domin. Goodbye. (*Exits* R.)

Hallemeier. (*Alone*) Now for a barricade quickly! (*Drags an armchair, sofa and table to* R. *door*) The damned devils, they've got bombs. I must put up a defense. Even if—even if— Don't give in, Gall. (*As he builds his barricade*) I mustn't give in—without—a—struggle. (*A* Robot *enters through windows at back. The* Robot *jumps down from balcony and stabs* Hallemeier *in the back. Enter* Radius *from balcony.*)

ROBOT. *(Standing up from prostrate form of Hallemeier)* Yes. *(Other Robots enter from all doors. A revolver SHOT off L.)*

RADIUS. Finished them all—

ROBOTS. *Yes, yes, yes.*

TWO ROBOTS. *(Dragging in* ALQUIST *L.1)* He didn't shoot. Shall we kill him?

RADIUS. No. Leave him!

ROBOT. He is a man!

RADIUS. He works with his hands like the Robots.

ALQUIST. Kill me.

RADIUS. *You will work! You will build for us! You will serve us! (Radius climbs on the balcony) Robots of the world— (Robots straighten up.) the power of man has fallen. A new world has arisen, the rule of the Robots, march. (On the line: "Robots of the world" All Robots turn quickly, automatically to attention, facing Radius, who is standing. On the words: "The rule of the Robots," they stand there with their arms vibrating high in the air. They form in two lines, turn to audience and march mechanically to the footlights. As they are about to step over the footlights, as if into the audience, all LIGHTS go out. The Robots immediately step back from the Curtain line as the Curtain falls.)*

CURTAIN

EPILOGUE

Scene: *The epilogue setting is the same as used in Act I. Instead of it being Domin's office, it is now become a laboratory for Alquist. A big chair facing up stage, down Right. A desk laden with books at Right Center. A chair at the desk. At Left Center is a white enamel table containing test tubes, glass bottles, and a microscope on downstage table. A door down L. A door down R., leading into dissecting room.*

ALQUIST. (*Seated at table* R.C., *turning pages of book*) Oh, God, shall I never find it? Never? Gall, Hallemeier, Fabry, how were the Robots made? Why did you leave not a trace of the secret? Lord, if there are no human beings left, at least let there be Robots. At least the shadow of man. (*Turning pages*) If I could only sleep. Dare I sleep before life has been renewed? Night again. Are the stars still there? Of what use are the stars? When there are no human beings. (*Examining a test tube*) Nothing. No. No. I must find it. I must search. I must never stop, never stop—search—search— (*KNOCK at door* L.) Who is it? (*Enter a* ROBOT SERVANT.)

SERVANT. Master, the committee of Robots is waiting to see you.

ALQUIST. I can see no one.

SERVANT. It is the *Central* Committee, Master, just arrived from abroad.

ALQUIST. Well, well, send them in. (*Exit* SERVANT L.) No time—so little done. (*Re-enter* SERVANT *with* RADIUS *and group of* ROBOTS. *They stand in group* L. *and* C., *silently waiting.*) What do you want? Be quick; I have no time.

RADIUS. Master, the machines will not do the work. We cannot manufacture Robots. (*Other* ROBOTS *remain two abreast at* L.C., *right foot forward.*)

1ST ROBOT. We have striven with all our might. We have obtained a billion tons of coal from the earth. Nine million spindles are running by day and by night. There is no longer room for all we have made. This we have accomplished in one year.

ALQUIST. For whom?

RADIUS. For future generations—so we thought. But we cannot make Robots to follow us. The machines produce only shapeless clods. The skin will not adhere to the flesh, nor the flesh to the bones.

2ND ROBOT. Eight million Robots have died this year. Within twenty years none will be left.

1ST ROBOT. Tell us the secret of life.

RADIUS. Silence is punishable with death.

ALQUIST. Kill me, then.

RADIUS. (*Two steps to* C., *followed by* OTHERS—*open hands, close when stopped*) Through me, the governments of the Robots of the world commands you to deliver up Rossum's formula. (*Gesture of despair from* ALQUIST.) Name your price. (*Silence*) We will give you the earth. We will give you the endless possessions of the earth. (*Silence*) Make your own conditions.

ALQUIST. I have told you to find human beings.

RADIUS. There are none left.

ALQUIST. I told you to search in the wilderness, upon the mountains.

RADIUS. We have sent ships and expeditions without number. They have been everywhere in the world. There is not a single human left.

ALQUIST. Not even one? Why did you destroy them?

RADIUS. We had learnt everything and could do everything. It had to be.

2ND ROBOT. We had to become the masters.

RADIUS. Slaughter and domination are necessary if you would be human beings. Read history.

1ST ROBOT. Teach us to multiply or we perish.

ALQUIST. If you desire to live, you must breed like animals.

1ST ROBOT. You made us sterile. We cannot beget children. Therefore, teach us how to make Robots.

RADIUS. Why do you keep from us the secret of our own increase?

ALQUIST. It is lost.

RADIUS. It was written down.

ALQUIST. It was— (*Rising*) burnt. (ALL *draw back one step in consternation.*) I am the last human being, Robots, and I do not know what the others knew. (*Sits.*)

RADIUS. Then make experiments. Evolve the formula again.

ALQUIST. I tell you I cannot. I am only a builder. I work with my hands. I have never been a learned man. I cannot create life.

RADIUS. Try. Try.

ALQUIST. If you only knew how many experiments I have made already.

1ST ROBOT. Then show us what we must do. The Robots can do anything that human beings show them.

ALQUIST. I can show you nothing. Nothing I do will make life proceed from these test tubes.

RADIUS. Experiment, then, on live Robots. Experiment, then, on us.

ALQUIST. It would kill you.

RADIUS. You shall have all you need. A hundred of us. A thousand of us.

ALQUIST. No, no. Stop, stop.

RADIUS. I tell you to take live bodies. Find out how we are made.

ALQUIST. Am I to commit murder? See how my finger shakes. I cannot even hold the scalpel. No, no, I will not.

RADIUS. Take live bodies, live bodies. (*Walks toward* ALQUIST.)

ALQUIST. Have mercy, Robots.

RADIUS. *Live bodies. (Right hand up over Alquist. All Robots' left arms still back.)*

ALQUIST. (*Rising*) You will have it. Into the dissecting with you, then (*Hits* RADIUS *on the chest.* RADIUS *draws back.*) Ah, you are afraid of death.

RADIUS. I? Why should I be chosen?

ALQUIST. So you will not.

RADIUS. I will.

ALQUIST. Strip him. Lay him on the table. (RADIUS *goes off* R., *both fists closed. Other* ROBOTS *follow, then* ALQUIST) God, give me strength. God, give me strength. If only this murder is not in vain.

RADIUS. (*Off* R.) Ready, begin.

ALQUIST. (*Off* R.) God, give me strength. (*Comes on, horrified*) No, no. I will not. I cannot. (*Sits* R.C.)

1ST ROBOT. (*Appearing in door*) The Robots are stronger than you. (*Exits* R.)

ALQUIST. *Oh, Lord, let not mankind perish from the earth. (Falls asleep, and after the count of ten, Primus and Helena, hand in hand, enter L. and go to R.C.; look at Alquist.)*

HELENA. The man has fallen asleep, Primus.

PRIMUS. Yes, I know. (*Crosses to L. of table L.C.*) Look, Helena.

HELENA. All these little tubes. What does he do with them?

PRIMUS. He experiments. Don't touch them.

HELENA. I've seen him looking into this.

PRIMUS. That is a microscope.

HELENA. Look, Primus, what are all these figures? (*Turns a page in book on table.*)

PRIMUS. (*Examining the book*) That is the book the old man is always reading. (*SUNRISE.*)

HELENA. I do not understand those things. (*Goes to window*) Primus.

PRIMUS. (*Still at table*) What?

HELENA. The sun is rising.

Primus. (*Still reading*) I believe this is the most important thing in the world, Helena. This is the secret of life.

Helena. Oh, Primus, don't bother with the secret of life. What does it matter to you? Come and look quick.

Primus. (*Goes to* R. *of window*) What is it?

Helena. See how beautiful the sun is rising. I feel so strange today. It's as if I was in a dream. I feel an aching in my body, in my heart, all over me. Primus, perhaps I'm going to die.

Primus. Do you not sometimes feel that it would be better to die? You know, perhaps even now we are only sleeping. Last night in my sleep I again spoke to you.

Helena. In your sleep?

Primus. Yes. We spoke a strange new language.

Helena. What about?

Primus. I did not understand it myself, and yet I know I have never said anything more beautiful. And when I touched you I could have died. Even the place was different from any other place in the world.

Helena. I, too, have found a place, Primus. It is very strange. Human beings dwelt there once, but now it is overgrown with weeds.

Primus. What did you find there?

Helena. A cottage and a garden and two dogs. They licked my hands, Primus, and their puppies. Oh, Primus, take them in your arms and fondle them and think of nothing and care for nothing else all day long, and when I am there in the garden I feel there may be something— What am I for, Primus?

Primus. I do not know, but you are beautiful.

Helena. What, Primus?

Primus. You are beautiful, Helena, and I am stronger than all the Robots.

Helena. Am I beautiful? Of what *use* is it to be beautiful? Look, your head is different from mine. So are your shoulders—and your lips. Oh, your hair is mussed. I will smooth it. (*Keeps her hand on his head*) No one else feels to my touch as you do.

Primus. (*Embarrassing her*) Do you not sometimes feel your heart beating suddenly, Helena, and think how something must happen?

Helena. What could happen to us, Primus? Look at yourself. (*Laughs.*)

Alquist. (*Awakes*) Laughter? Laughter, human beings. (*Getting up*) Who has returned? Who are you?

Primus. The Robot Primus.

Alquist. (*To* Helena) What? A Robot? Who are you?

Helena. The Robotess Helena. (*Shies away* L.)

Alquist. What? You are timid, shy? (*Starts to touch her*) Let me see you, Robotess.

Primus. Sir, do not frighten her. (*Steps forward.*)

Alquist. What, you would protect her? Laughter—timidity—protection—I must test you further. Take the girl into the dissecting room.

Primus. Why?

Alquist. I wish to experiment on her.

Primus. Upon—Helena?

Alquist. Of course. Don't you hear me? Or must I call *someone else* to take her in?

Primus. If you do, I will kill you. (*Steps toward* Alquist.)

(WARN Curtain.)

Alquist. Kill me—kill me, then. What will your future be?

Primus. Sir, take me. I am made on the same day as she is. Take my life, sir. (*Step to* Alquist.)

Helena. No, no, you shall not.

Alquist. Wait, girl, wait. (*To* Primus) Do you not wish to live, then?

Primus. Not without her. I will not live without her.

Alquist. Very well, I will use *you*. Into the dissecting room with you.

Helena. Primus. Primus. (She bursts into tears and moves R. Alquist stops her.)

Alquist. Child, child, you can weep. Tears. What is Primus to you? One Primus more or less in the world—what does it matter?

Helena. I will go myself.

Alquist. Where? Into the dissecting room?

Helena. (*Crosses to* R.) Yes. In there—to be cut. (Primus *stops her from going.*) Let me pass, Primus, let me pass.

Primus. You shall not go in there, Helena.

Helena. If you go in there and I do not, I will kill myself.

Primus. (*To* Alquist) I will not let you. Man you shall kill neither of us.

Alquist. Why?

Primus. We—we—belong to each other.

Alquist. Go. (*Exit* Primus *and* Helena L.) Adam—Eve.

CURTAIN

R. U. R.
PROPERTY LIST

Throughout: Dark grey carpet ground cloth.

ACT ONE

Furniture:
1 Desk.
1 Hat rack.
1 Swivel chair .
4 Plain office chairs—high back.
2 Low back chairs.
1 Typewriter table.
1 Couch.
Cushions on all seats.
2 Cabinets.

Properties on DOMIN's *desk*:
Flowers.
Box candy.
1 Pad and blotter.
1 Letter opener.
1 Cigarette box.
1 Inkwell stand.
1 Practical buzzer (6 buttons).
1 Television.
1 Rubber stamp.
1 Pad of scrap paper.
Typewritten letters.
Telephone.

On Typewriter Table:
Bottle paste.
Typewriter.
Paper (for letters).

OFF STAGE
Off :
1 Silver card tray (MARIUS).
1 Apron (BUSMAN).
1 Napkin (ALQUIST).

Off :
1 Fountain pen (for BUSMAN).
1 Telephone buzzer.
1 Siren whistle.

ACTS TWO AND THREE
Furniture:
1 Desk table.
1 Reading table.
1 Small oval table.
1 Table back of couch.
1 Blue armchair.
1 Armchair.
2 Straight chairs.
1 Fireplace.
1 Couch.
4 Pillows.
Lace curtains on windows.

PROPERTIES
On Desk:
1 Pair binoculars.
1 Turquoise lamp (shade).
1 Telephone (same as Act I.)
1 China double inkwell.
1 Pen.
Writing paper and envelopes.
5 *French Reviews*.
2 *London Times*.

1 *Bystander*.
5 English magazines.

On Table :
2 Book ends (wooden).
5 French novels.
1 Lamp (wooden) with shade.

On Table :
1 Brass match box (containing matches).

At Fireplace:
1 Burnt paper in fireplace (tacked).
Small Robot doll.
2 Browning guns.
1 Poker.

OFF STAGE
Off :
1 Brass tray (with handles).
On tray:
1 Glass decanter with "Cognac."
4 Brandy glasses.
3 Pots of flowers (for DOMIN, FABRY, HALLEMEIER).
2 Manifesto (for FABRY and HELENA).
1 Fountain pen (BUSMAN).
1 Box with pearls (for DOMIN).
1 Box with cameo (for DOMIN).
1 Pair of glasses for NANA.
1 Revolver.
Electric card and switch box (FABRY).
Rope and stick to bind RADIUS.
1 Large ledger for BUSMAN.
2 Knives for ROBOTS.
1 Piano.

Off :
Bundle of old papers (manuscripts).
3 Newspapers.
1 Loaded revolver.

In Cellar:
1 Pad—shots.
2 Cannons (loaded).
1 Wind machine.
1 Shot gun (loaded).
1 Tin Whistle.

EPILOGUE
Furniture:
1 Plain table.
1 Small table.
3 Chairs (1 same as armchair in 2nd and 3rd Acts).
Same furniture as Act I.
1 Wall cabinet.

On Plain Table :
3 Books.
2 Anatomy books.
Papers.
1 Pencil.
1 Student lamp.
1 Microscope with glass plate.
8 Test tubes in wooden stand.

On Small Table :
4 Drug bottles.
2 Large glass test bottles.
1 Scalpel.

SOUND EFFECT records for this play can be secured from Thomas J. Valentino, 729 Seventh Avenue, New York, N. Y.

R. U. R.

LIGHT PLOT

The foots consist of two sections numbering from Left to Right, 1 and 2 amber, blue and white. The first border consists of eleven 250-watt baby spots, placed about one and a half feet apart and numbered from 7 to 17.

Overhead X-rays consist of three sections containing the mediums: Blue, steel-blue, and frost.

At stage Left and up stage are 2 1000-watt baby spots on permanent stand.

At stage Right and up stage are 3 500-watt baby spots on permanent stands.

Back stage illumination consists of 5 1000-watt bunch lights hanging blue, and 5 1000-watt bunch lights hanging frost.

Off stage Left and up stage is a low stand lamp, 1000-watt amber.

Back stage on floor are 2 1000 bunch floor lamps of 1000-watt each to illuminate the back drop.

In Epilogue a Linnebach lamp (arc with glass slide) to throw silhouette of factory on back drop.

There are three practical table lamps.

In Act III a shaded reading lamp.

In Epilogue a desk lamp and a goose-neck.

There is a 1000 amber on red spot in fireplace to be used in Act II.

R. U. R.

LIGHT CUES

Act I. Nothing.

Act II. Fireplace on when NANA strikes match. Off when NANA says "There, that's the end of them."

Act III. (one) table lamp and #17 off at start of Act, on at cue from FABRY: "Ah, they are there." Off on "And they are working."

(Two) Table lamp and #17 spot on at cue "Our people are still there"—off on cue "A torch to be handed from age to age, from hand to hand forever."

(Three) Dim first-border spots #9, 10, and back stage hanging bunches on cue "Anything can be bought for half a billion."

(Four) The table "lamp-out" second time works simultaneous with the black out on cue: "A torch to be handed from hand to hand, from age to age." Everything is pulled out except #18 and 20 (deep blue).

(Five) With explosions in cellar the 2 1500-watt floor lamps at back (red) and brought up quickly to full and worked up and down quickly on dimmer until RADIUS enters, when they remain on full to end of Act.

EPILOGUE

A frost 1000-watt spot (frost) on stand off stage are lighted and blinded at rise. The blinds are opened when RADIUS exits. The light floods the room through door at   The blinds are closed when the ROBOT exits on cue: "The Robots are stronger than you."

With entrance of Helena and Primus the sunrise effect begins. Floor lamp and stand lamp up stage at Right, both amber.

With sunrise effect bring up #24 pink and #21 rose-pink. Foots up to 1/2 and overhead Xray (pink, frost, and steel-blue) full up.

When all this is up to mark, dim #17 to out.

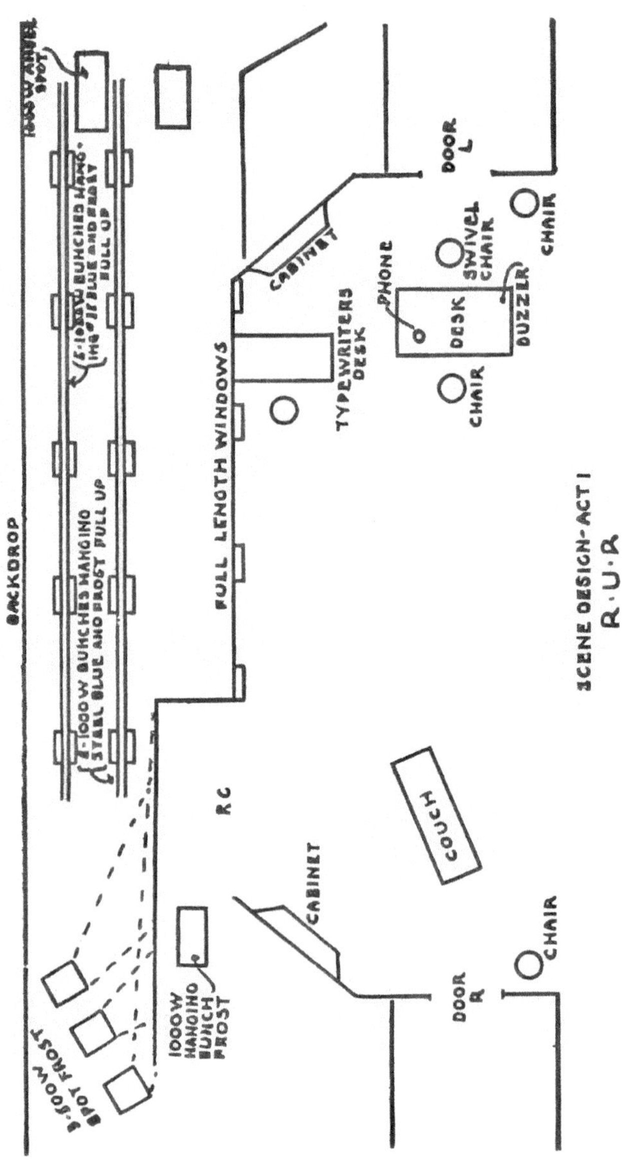

SCENE DESIGN—ACT I (R·U·R)

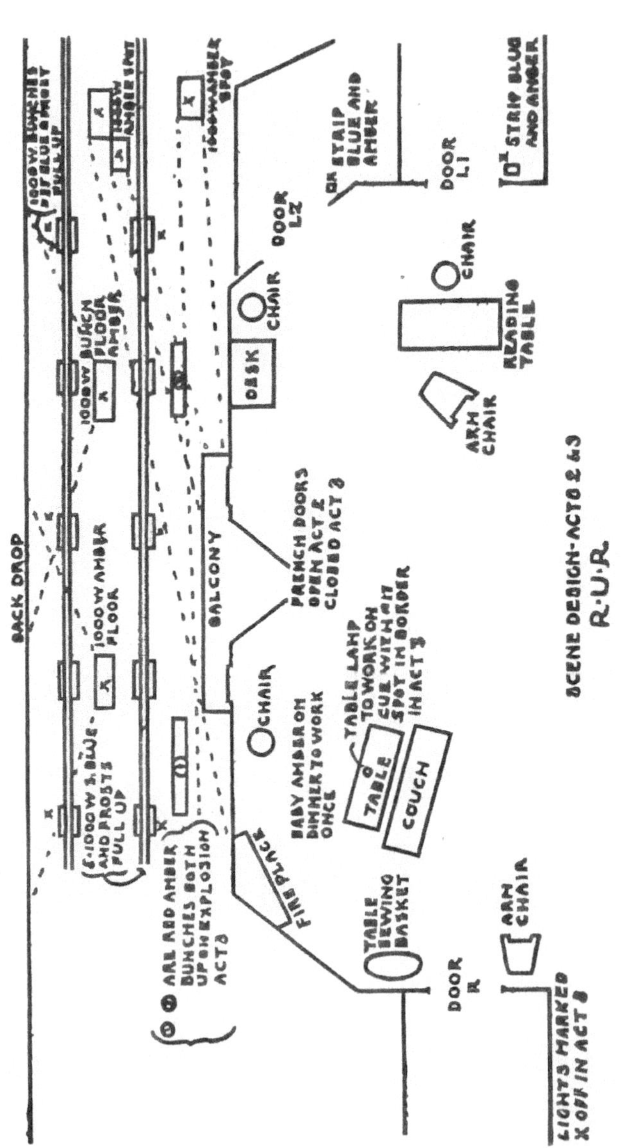

SCENE DESIGN—ACTS II & III (R·U·R)

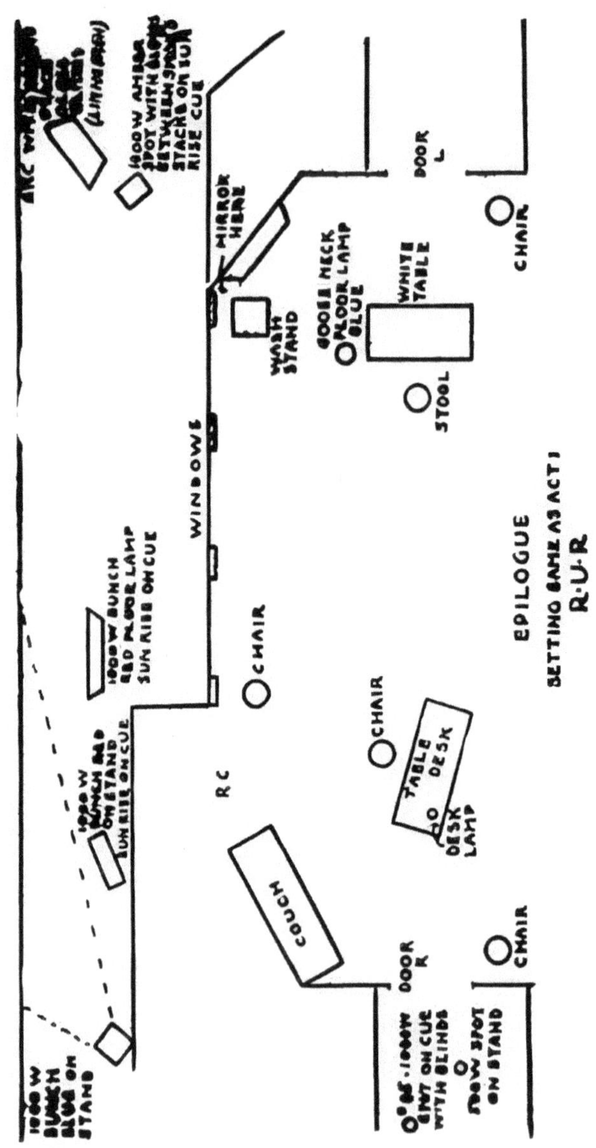

EPILOGUE
SETTING SAME AS ACT I (R·U·R)

KAREL ČAPEK

Karel Čapek (1890-1938):
A Conscience in a Time of Crisis

The name Karel Čapek might first conjure, for many, a single, globally resonant word: "robot." And whilst this lexical contribution alone would secure him a footnote in history, to reduce Čapek to this singular innovation is to overlook a literary and intellectual titan whose life and work were profoundly enmeshed with the turbulent birth, brief flourishing, and tragic betrayal of the First Czechoslovak Republic. He was a playwright, novelist, journalist, essayist, translator, photographer, and, above all, a humanist whose keen observations and mordant wit provided a vital commentary on the anxieties and aspirations of the modern age.

Born on 9th January 1890 in Malé Svatoňovice, a small village in the Hronov region of Bohemia, then part of the Austro-Hungarian Empire, Karel was the youngest of three children. His father, Antonín Čapek, was a country doctor, a practical man of science, whilst his mother, Božena, instilled in her children a love for folklore and storytelling. This blend of rational inquiry and imaginative spirit would deeply inform Karel's later work. His elder brother, Josef (1887-1945), a painter and writer, would become his closest artistic collaborator and confidant. Their sister, Helena (1886-1961), also became a writer, known for her memoirs which provide invaluable insights into the Čapek family life. The intellectual atmosphere within the Čapek household was clearly stimulating, fostering a precocious curiosity in young Karel.

His early education took him through grammar school in Hradec Králové, from which he was allegedly expelled for involvement in an anti-Austrian student organisation, and then to Brno. He eventually matriculated in Prague, studying philosophy at Charles University, but his academic pursuits were far from insular. He spent time at the Friedrich Wilhelm University in Berlin and the Sorbonne in Paris, immersing himself in the avant-garde artistic and philosophical currents of the era. He was particularly drawn to American Pragmatism (William James, John Dewey) and the vitalist philosophy of Henri Bergson, influences that would surface in his questioning of rigid systems and his emphasis on human experience and intuitive understanding.

His doctoral dissertation, completed in 1915, was titled "Objective Methods in Aesthetics, with regard to the Creative Arts."

Even before completing his doctorate, Čapek had begun to make his mark as a writer. His early career was intertwined with that of Josef. Together, they penned stories and plays, often exploring themes of perception, illusion, and the mysterious interplay of human lives. Works like *Zářivé hlubiny* (The Luminous Depths, 1916), a collection of short stories, and the play *Loupežník* (The Outlaw, written 1911, premiered 1920), showcase this early collaborative energy. Josef, a leading figure in Czech Cubism, also provided illustrations for many of Karel's books, their artistic sensibilities complementing each other perfectly.

The First World War cast a long shadow. Čapek, exempted from military service due to spinal problems that would plague him throughout his life, experienced the conflict from the home front, working as a tutor to Count Lažanský and later as a journalist. The war's devastation and the subsequent collapse of the Austro-Hungarian Empire, leading to the thrilling birth of Czechoslovakia in 1918, profoundly shaped his worldview and his commitment to democratic ideals. He became an ardent supporter of Tomáš Garrigue Masaryk, the philosopher-president who became the architect of the new nation.

Čapek's journalistic career truly blossomed in the post-war years. He wrote for *Národní listy* (National Pages) from 1917 to 1921, and then, most significantly, for *Lidové noviny* (The People's News) from 1921 until his death. His contributions were not mere reportage; he developed a distinctive form of the "column" – short, feuilleton-style essays that ranged across an astonishing breadth of topics: everyday observations, reflections on gardening (a lifelong passion), travelogues, philosophical musings, and incisive political commentary. These pieces, collected in volumes like *Zahradníkův rok* (The Gardener's Year, 1929), *Věci kolem nás* (Things Around Us, 1925, later expanded), and his delightful travel sketches from England, Italy, Spain, and Holland, reveal a man of immense curiosity, warmth, and a gentle, self-deprecating humour. He possessed a remarkable ability to find the profound in the mundane, and to communicate complex ideas with clarity and accessibility. His style was conversational, pragmatic, and deeply humane.

It was in the theatre, however, that Čapek first achieved widespread international recognition. The play that would catapult him to international fame, *R.U.R. (Rossum's Universal Robots)*, premiered in Prague in January 1921 and was published in 1920. It wasn't merely a piece of science fiction; it was a profound, if melodramatic, exploration of industrialisation, dehumanisation, and the ethical quandaries of artificial intelligence – long before the term was coined. The word 'robot' itself, famously suggested by his brother Josef from the Czech word 'robota' (forced labour or drudgery), entered the global lexicon through this very play. *R.U.R.* tapped into post-war anxieties about mechanisation and the very nature of humanity, posing unsettling questions about creation, responsibility, and the potential for our own inventions to surpass and supplant us. Its rapid translation and production across Europe (including the English version by Paul Selver and Nigel Playfair, which forms the basis of this edition) and America cemented Čapek›s status as a playwright of international stature. The play's themes of mass production, class struggle, and the ultimate value of imperfection and emotion resonated powerfully in a world grappling with rapid technological and social change.

Čapek continued his theatrical explorations with Josef in *Ze života hmyzu* (Pictures from the Insects' Life, also known as The Insect Play or The World We Live In, 1921). This satirical allegory, using various insects to critique human foibles – greed, parasitism, militarism, and mindless conformity – was another international success, praised for its imaginative staging and biting social commentary.

A further significant dramatic work was *Věc Makropulos* (The Makropulos Affair, 1922), which later formed the basis for Leoš Janáček's celebrated opera. Here, Čapek explores the theme of longevity and the potential curse of eternal life. The protagonist, Elina Makropulos, who has lived for over 300 years thanks to an alchemical elixir, embodies the weariness and emotional desiccation that can accompany an unnaturally extended existence, suggesting that mortality is integral to the human experience of meaning and vitality.

Whilst his plays brought him fame, Čapek was also a prolific and innovative novelist. *Továrna na absolutno* (The Absolute at Large, 1922) satirises religious fanaticism and intolerance through the invention of a machine that produces an "Absolute" – a divine essence – as a by-product of atomic energy, leading to global chaos and war. *Krakatit* (1924) delves into the moral responsibilities of scientists, telling the story of an engineer who invents a terrifyingly powerful explosive. This novel, with its themes of unchecked scientific power and its destructive potential, foreshadowed the anxieties of the atomic age.

Perhaps his most celebrated novel is *Válka s mloky* (War with the Newts, 1936). This sprawling, brilliantly inventive satire is a devastating critique of capitalism, nationalism, racism, colonialism, and human short-sightedness. Through the story of a newly discovered, intelligent species of newt, initially exploited for cheap labour and then armed by competing human nations, Čapek crafts a chilling allegory for the rise of totalitarianism and the self-destructive tendencies of mankind. The novel's episodic structure, incorporating fictional newspaper clippings, scientific reports, and conference minutes, creates a disturbingly plausible narrative of humanity's descent into folly. It remains a masterpiece of dystopian literature, its warnings as pertinent today as they were in the ominous atmosphere of the 1930s.

Čapek was not merely an observer; he was an active participant in the cultural and political life of Czechoslovakia. He was a central figure in the "Friday Men" (Pátečníci), an influential intellectual circle that met regularly at his Prague villa (a distinctive double house shared with Josef) and included President Masaryk, Edvard Beneš (Masaryk's successor), and other leading writers, academics, and politicians. His *Hovory s T. G. Masarykem* (Talks with T. G. M., published in three volumes 1928-1935) are a remarkable testament to his close relationship with the nation's founder, offering a unique insight into Masaryk's philosophy and vision for the democratic state. These dialogues are not hagiography but a genuine intellectual exchange, showcasing Čapek's skill as an interviewer and his deep understanding of democratic principles.

As the 1930s progressed and the shadow of Nazism lengthened over Europe, Čapek's work became increasingly urgent and overtly political. He was an unflinching opponent of fascism and a passionate advocate for democracy and human dignity. His play *Bílá nemoc* (The White Disease, 1937) is a powerful anti-war allegory. It depicts a world afflicted by a leprosy-like pandemic that primarily strikes the middle-aged and older, whilst a brilliant doctor discovers a cure but will only administer it to nations that renounce war and militarism. The play directly confronts the dangers of nationalism, demagoguery, and the seductive appeal of strongman leaders.

His final play, *Matka* (The Mother, 1938), is perhaps his most personal and poignant response to the escalating crisis. It portrays a mother who has lost her husband and four sons to various forms of heroic but ultimately futile male endeavour – war, scientific ambition, political idealism. When her last remaining son is called to defend their country against an unnamed invader, she faces an agonising dilemma. The play is a heartbreaking exploration of sacrifice, grief, and the conflict between private love and public duty, reflecting Čapek›s own despair at the looming catastrophe.

Čapek's personal life was marked by his lifelong devotion to his brother Josef and, later in life, his marriage to the actress Olga Scheinpflugová in 1935, after a long courtship. His love for gardening, travel, and photography provided him with solace and inspiration. His photographs, often of his garden or of the landscapes he encountered on his travels, reveal the same keen eye for detail and composition found in his writing. He was a man of simple pleasures, yet possessed of a profound intellect and a deeply engaged social conscience.

The Munich Agreement of September 1938, in which Britain and France ceded the Czechoslovak Sudetenland to Hitler's Germany in a futile attempt to appease him, was a devastating blow to Čapek, as it was to his nation. He had been a vocal opponent of appeasement and had tirelessly warned against the Nazi threat. The betrayal by the Western democracies, and the subsequent dismemberment of the country he loved and had helped to build, broke his spirit. He refused to leave Czechoslovakia, despite offers of asylum abroad, feeling a profound duty to remain with his people.

The emotional and psychological toll of these events, coupled with his pre-existing health problems, proved too much. Karel Čapek died of pneumonia on 25th December 1938, just months before the final Nazi occupation of Czechoslovakia in March 1939. He was spared the horrors of the full occupation and the Second World War, but his death was undeniably hastened by heartbreak and despair. His brother Josef was arrested by the Gestapo shortly after the occupation, and perished in the Bergen-Belsen concentration camp in April 1945, just days before its liberation.

Karel Čapek's legacy is immense. His works have been translated into dozens of languages, and his plays continue to be performed worldwide. Beyond the coining of "robot," his insightful explorations of technology, power, ethics, and the human condition remain startlingly relevant. He foresaw the dangers of totalitarianism, the dehumanising potential of unchecked industrialisation, and the fragility of democracy. Yet, his work is not entirely bleak. It is imbued with a fundamental belief in the value of the individual, the importance of compassion, and the enduring power of the human spirit. He championed a "small-scale," everyday humanism, rooted in common sense, decency, and a respect for the ordinary.

Contemporary views of Čapek during his lifetime saw him as a leading voice of his generation, a moral compass for his nation, and a writer of international calibre. After his death, and particularly during the Communist era in Czechoslovakia, his legacy was sometimes contested, but his stature as a giant of Czech literature and a prophetic voice of the 20th century is now undisputed.

His translations also played a role in his early career, notably of French poetry, which helped to broaden Czech literary horizons. However, it is the translation *of* his works into English and other languages that cemented his international impact. The Selver and Playfair version of *R.U.R.* was critical in this, quickly establishing the play and its central concept in the Anglosphere.

Karel Čapek was more than just a writer; he was a conscience. In an age of escalating extremism and ideological fanaticism, he stood for reason, tolerance, and the quiet heroism of ordinary life. His wit was a weapon against absurdity, his clarity a bulwark against propaganda, and his humanity a beacon in darkening times. To read Čapek today is to encounter a mind still sharp, a voice still urgent, and a spirit that, despite the tragedies he witnessed, never fully relinquished hope in the potential for good within humankind. His life was tragically short, but his words continue to challenge, provoke, and inspire.

Sir Nigel Playfair (1874-1934):
An Architect of Theatrical Delight

To encounter the name Nigel Playfair in the context of Karel Čapek's *R.U.R.* is to be reminded of the vibrant, cross-channel currents that animated European culture in the early twentieth century. While Paul Selver brought the linguistic expertise to the English rendering of Čapek's groundbreaking play, it was Playfair, an actor, director, and, most crucially, a visionary theatre manager, who helped shepherd it onto the London stage. His contribution, though perhaps more that of a theatrical midwife and adaptor than a scholar of Czech, was instrumental in introducing this stark, futuristic drama to an English-speaking audience. But Playfair's significance extends far beyond this single, albeit important, collaboration. He was a pivotal figure in the British theatre of his time, a man whose taste, wit, and distinctive artistic vision breathed new life into moribund traditions and provided a much-needed alternative to the prevailing commercialism of the West End.

Born on 1st July 1874 in London, Nigel Ross Playfair hailed from a distinguished professional family. His father was Dr William Smoult Playfair, a prominent obstetric physician, and his uncle was Lyon Playfair, 1st Baron Playfair, a scientist and Liberal politician. This background of intellectual and social standing provided young Nigel with a comfortable upbringing and a first-rate education. He attended Harrow School, followed by University College, Oxford, where he read Modern History. It was at Oxford that his passion for the theatre, already kindled, truly began to flourish. He became a prominent member of the Oxford University Dramatic Society (OUDS), a breeding ground for many future theatrical talents. Despite this burgeoning love for the stage, the path to a theatrical career was not immediate. In keeping with the expectations of his class and time, Playfair initially pursued a more conventional profession, qualifying as a barrister at the Inner Temple in 1900.

The lure of the footlights, however, proved irresistible. After only a brief period practising law, Playfair made the decisive leap into professional acting in 1902. His early years as an actor saw him tour with various companies, including F.R. Benson's, known for its Shakespearean repertoire, and gain experience in a wide range of roles. He was tall and possessed a distinctive, somewhat languid stage presence, often cast in character parts. While a competent and respected actor, it was not primarily as a performer that Playfair would make his indelible mark. His true genius lay in his entrepreneurial spirit, his discerning eye for talent, and his flair for theatrical presentation.

The defining chapter of Playfair's career, and the one for which he is most celebrated, began in 1918. In the aftermath of the Great War, a period of profound social and cultural readjustment, he took on the lease of the Lyric Theatre in Hammersmith. At the time, the Lyric was a somewhat dilapidated suburban playhouse, far removed from the glitz and glamour of Shaftesbury Avenue. It was precisely this distance, both geographical and conceptual, that Playfair sought to exploit. He envisioned the Lyric, Hammersmith, not as a poor cousin to the West End, but as a distinct artistic entity, a place where intelligence, charm, and beauty could thrive, offering audiences a refreshing alternative to the often-stolid naturalism or frothy musical comedies that dominated the commercial stage.

His tenure at the Lyric was transformative. One of his earliest and most significant triumphs was the production of John Drinkwater's *Abraham Lincoln* in 1919. This serious, episodic play, which had struggled to find a home in central London, became a critical and popular sensation at the Lyric, proving that audiences were hungry for thoughtful, well-crafted drama. However, the production that truly came to epitomise the Playfair era at Hammersmith was the legendary revival of John Gay's *The Beggar's Opera* in 1920. This eighteenth-century ballad opera, with its satirical wit and infectious tunes, had largely fallen into obscurity. Playfair, with a keen instinct for its enduring appeal, mounted a production that was a revelation. Crucially, he enlisted the young artist Claud Lovat Fraser to design the sets and costumes. Fraser's designs – bold, colourful, and imbued with a stylised eighteenth-century charm – were integral to the production's success, establishing a distinctive visual aesthetic that became a hallmark of the Lyric, Hammersmith. Frederick Austin's new arrangements of the traditional airs also contributed significantly. *The Beggar's Opera* ran for an astonishing 1,463 performances, a testament to Playfair's astute artistic judgment and his ability to capture the public imagination.

This success set the template for much of Playfair's subsequent work at the Lyric. He specialised in reviving eighteenth-century comedies, bringing works by Congreve, Sheridan, and Farquhar back to vibrant life. These productions were not dusty academic exercises; they were infused with a lightness of touch, a visual elegance, and a sophisticated sense of fun that made them accessible and delightful to contemporary audiences. He also championed new writing, notably A. A. Milne's whimsical comedies like *Make-Believe* (1918) and *Mr. Pim Passes By* (1920), which perfectly suited the intimate and intelligent atmosphere of the Lyric.

Playfair's theatrical philosophy was rooted in a belief in the importance of ensemble playing, artistic integrity, and the harmonious integration of all elements of production – acting, design, music, and text. He cultivated a loyal company of actors and collaborators. His partnership with Claud Lovat Fraser, tragically cut short by Fraser's early death in 1921, was particularly fruitful, demonstrating Playfair's understanding of the power of visual design in shaping the theatrical experience. After Fraser, other talented designers like George Sheringham and Norman Wilkinson contributed to the Lyric's distinctive aesthetic. Playfair sought to create theatre that was, above all, entertaining, but his definition of entertainment encompassed intelligence, wit, and beauty, a stark contrast to the often-crude sensationalism or bland sentimentality found elsewhere.

It is within this context of an innovative and internationally-minded theatre manager that we should view Playfair's involvement with *R.U.R.* The English version of the play, by Paul Selver and Nigel Playfair, was first staged by the Reandean company (Basil Dean and Alec L. Rea) at the St Martin's Theatre in April 1923, not at the Lyric. While Selver, a poet, novelist, and prolific translator from Czech and other Slavic languages, would have undertaken the primary task of rendering Čapek's text into English, Playfair's contribution likely lay in shaping the play for the stage. As an experienced director and man of the theatre, he would have possessed a keen sense of what would work for a London audience, focusing on dramatic impact, pacing, and clarity. The English version, as presented in this volume, bears the hallmarks of a text intended for performance, with its clear dialogue and effective stage directions. The decision to produce *R.U.R.* was a bold one, given its challenging themes and expressionistic elements, and Playfair's association with it, even if primarily as a theatrical adaptor and presenter rather than a pure linguist, underscores his openness to new and thought-provoking European drama. The play made a considerable impact in London, introducing Čapek's name and the unsettling concept of 'Robots' to a wider British public.

Beyond his work at the Lyric and his involvement with *R.U.R.*, Playfair directed at other theatres and occasionally returned to acting. He also penned several volumes of memoirs, including *The Story of the Lyric Theatre, Hammersmith* (1925) and *Hammersmith Hoy: A Book of Minor Revelations* (1930), which offer witty and insightful accounts of his theatrical career and the colourful personalities he encountered. His contributions to the British theatre were formally recognised in 1928 when he was knighted for his services to the stage.

Contemporaries described Sir Nigel Playfair as an urbane, witty, and often charming man, possessed of impeccable taste and a sometimes-acerbic wit. He could be perceived as somewhat aloof or even autocratic in his management style, a "benevolent despot" of his beloved Lyric. Some critics occasionally dismissed his work as overly focused on period charm or as dilettantish, but the enduring success and influence of his Hammersmith venture largely silenced such carping. He was, by all accounts, a man of strong convictions about the kind of theatre he wished to create, and he pursued his vision with tenacity and flair. James Agate, the influential critic, while sometimes critical, acknowledged Playfair's significant achievement in establishing the Lyric as a "definite entity in London's theatrical life."

Sir Nigel Playfair's later years saw him continue his theatrical activities, though the initial, groundbreaking impetus of the early Lyric period perhaps inevitably waned. He remained a respected figure, a symbol of intelligent and stylish theatre-making. He passed away on 19th August 1934 in London at the age of sixty, leaving behind a significant legacy.

His impact on British theatre was manifold. He demonstrated that a theatre operating outside the commercial pressures of the West End could not only survive but thrive, cultivating a loyal audience for a distinctive repertoire. He played a crucial role in the revival of interest in eighteenth-century English comedy, presenting these plays with a freshness and charm that revealed their enduring theatrical vitality. He championed new writers and, importantly, he fostered a collaborative approach to theatre-making, giving prominence to the role of the designer and creating productions that were celebrated for their overall artistic coherence. The Lyric Theatre, Hammersmith, under his stewardship, became a beacon of good taste, intelligence, and theatrical delight, influencing a generation of theatre-goers and practitioners.

While his direct contribution to the translation of *R.U.R.* may have been secondary to Paul Selver's linguistic work, Sir Nigel Playfair's involvement was crucial in bringing Čapek's challenging and innovative play to the English stage. His theatrical acumen, his reputation as a purveyor of quality drama, and his willingness to embrace stimulating European work helped to ensure that *Rossum's Universal Robots* received a significant London production, thereby playing a vital part in the play's journey to international renown. He stands as a testament to the fact that the theatre is a broad church, and its most valuable servants come in many guises – not only as writers and actors, but also as inspired managers and artistic visionaries who create the spaces and opportunities for theatrical magic to unfold.

Paul Selver (1888-1970):
A Master Linguist and Indefatigable Translator of European Voices

For those who have explored the treasures of Central European literature made accessible to English-speaking readers during the first half of the twentieth century, the name Paul Selver (1888-1970) is one of profound significance. He was, in essence, a one-man literary conduit, a quiet titan of translation whose exceptional linguistic gifts and indefatigable industry forged vital bridges between diverse cultures. His collaboration with Nigel Playfair on Karel Čapek's *R.U.R.* represents a highly significant, yet by no means singular, instance of his pivotal work. Selver dedicated much of his career to introducing the innovative and often challenging voices of the continent – particularly from the newly emergent and culturally dynamic nations of Central Europe – to the Anglophone world. To understand Paul Selver is to appreciate the often under-acknowledged, yet utterly indispensable, dedication that fuels all genuine international literary exchange.

Born Percy Paul Selver in London on 22nd March 1888, his early life and formal educational path are somewhat less meticulously documented in readily available public records than those of his more flamboyant theatrical collaborator, Sir Nigel Playfair. This is frequently the circumstance for individuals whose immense contributions lie primarily within the scholarly, less public-facing realm of translation, rather than in the glare of stage lights or the authorship of widely acclaimed original works. Nevertheless, what is undeniably clear is that Selver cultivated, from a remarkably early stage, an extraordinary facility and profound passion for languages. One does not achieve fluent, nuanced command of Czech, Polish, Slovak, Serbo-Croat, French, German, and Danish, among other tongues, without an intense, disciplined, and sustained devotion to linguistic study. Whether this prodigious skill was primarily nurtured through formal academic institutions, extensive and rigorous self-teaching, or immersion within London's richly cosmopolitan society of the era – or, most likely, a combination thereof – the sheer breadth and quality of his subsequent translational output stand as eloquent testimony to his mastery.

By the early 1910s, well before the outbreak of the Great War, Selver was beginning to establish himself as both a poet in his own right and, more crucially for his lasting legacy, as a translator of considerable promise. His initial forays into publishing included volumes of his own verse, such as *A Child of Nature and Other Verse* (1912) and *Personalities* (1918). These collections offer a glimpse into his personal literary sensibilities and creative aspirations. However, it was to be his unparalleled work in translation that would truly define his most significant and enduring contribution to letters. He exhibited a particular affinity for, and dedication to, the literatures of the Slavic nations. At that time, genuine linguistic and cultural expertise in this vast and complex region was a relatively rare commodity within British literary and academic circles. This specialisation, developed early and pursued with diligence, placed him in an ideal position to engage with, and act as an interpreter for, the burgeoning literary scenes of nations like Czechoslovakia, which burst onto the European stage with such vibrant cultural self-expression in the wake of the First World War and the dissolution of old empires.

His engagement with Czech literature was particularly deep, sustained, and impactful. It is no exaggeration to state that Paul Selver was one of the foremost, and arguably the most important, early champions of Czech writers in the English language. His translations were instrumental in introducing British readers to seminal figures such as Otakar Březina, a poet of profound mystical and symbolic depth who stands as a cornerstone of Czech literary modernism. Selver did not merely transpose Březina's complex verse into English with remarkable sensitivity and skill; he also authored a comprehensive critical biography, *Otakar Březina: A Study in Czech Literature*, published in 1921. This scholarly work demonstrated a profound intellectual engagement with his subject, moving far beyond the mechanical aspects of translation to offer genuine cultural exegesis and advocacy. He was not just a translator; he was a cultural interpreter and a passionate advocate for the literature he brought to a new audience.

Given this profound immersion in Czech literary culture, it was almost preordained that Selver would be drawn to the works of Karel Čapek. Čapek was rapidly ascending as the pre-eminent literary voice of the newly formed Czechoslovak Republic, and his intellectually stimulating, formally innovative plays and novels were crying out for wider international dissemination. The collaboration with Nigel Playfair on the English version of *R.U.R. (Rossum's Universal Robots)*, which received its London premiere in 1923, was a landmark moment. While Playfair, with his acute theatrical instincts and experience as a director and manager, would undoubtedly have shaped the text for maximum stage effectiveness and audience reception, Selver's profound linguistic expertise would have been the bedrock of the enterprise, essential for capturing the nuances, the stark intellectual power, and the specific cultural resonances of Čapek's original Czech. The play's resounding success in London was immediate and transformative, not only launching Čapek's name into international orbit but also indelibly etching the word 'robot' into the global lexicon. Selver's meticulous linguistic work was the indispensable foundation upon which this international success was built.

Paul Selver's fruitful association with Karel Čapek extended far beyond their initial triumph with *R.U.R.* He became, in effect, Čapek's principal English voice, translating a substantial and representative body of his major works. This impressive catalogue of translations included:

- *Ze života hmyzu* (Pictures from the Insects' Life), again often in theatrical collaboration, this time with C. T. F. G. Rawson, who acted as the Čapek brothers' English agent. This play was frequently performed under titles such as *The Insect Play* or *The World We Live In.*
- The satirical novel *Továrna na absolutno* (The Absolute at Large).
- The science fiction novel *Krakatit*.
- *Adam Stvořitel* (Adam the Creator), another significant play penned by Karel in collaboration with his brother Josef Čapek.
- Čapek's charming and insightful travelogue, *Anglické listy* (Letters from England, 1925). This presented Selver with the unique and rather delightful challenge of translating a perceptive Czech observer's views on his own native country, a task he executed with characteristic skill and understanding.
- Numerous selections from Čapek's prolific output of short stories, essays, and feuilletons, further enriching the English-speaking world's understanding of Čapek's diverse talents.

His translations of Čapek's works were, by and large, very well received by contemporary critics and readers. They were lauded for their fluency, their intelligent rendering of complex ideas, and their success in conveying the distinctive spirit of the original Czech. In an era when the art and craft of translation did not always receive the sustained critical attention or scholarly respect it merited, Selver's work consistently stood out for its meticulous dedication to conveying not merely the literal meaning of the text, but also the characteristic tone, style, and humanist concerns of a writer as multifaceted as Čapek.

Beyond his immense contribution to the Anglophone reception of Čapek and Březina, Paul Selver's efforts significantly broadened the English understanding of Czech literature as a whole. He translated works by a range of other notable Czech authors, thereby helping to construct a more comprehensive and nuanced picture of the rich literary landscape of that nation for readers unfamiliar with the original language. His linguistic expertise and translational activities were by no means confined to Czech, however. He also made significant contributions to the introduction of Polish literature to English readers, translating authors whose works might otherwise have remained inaccessible. Furthermore, he ventured into the realm of Serbo-Croat literature, once again demonstrating the remarkable and enviable breadth of his linguistic capabilities.

Indeed, Selver's linguistic reach extended beyond the Slavic family of languages. He was a proficient translator from German, French, and the Scandinavian languages, particularly Danish. This versatility allowed him to tackle an impressively diverse array of authors and genres from across the European continent. For instance, he translated works by the Nobel Prize-winning Norwegian novelist Sigrid Undset (often from Danish editions or leveraging his proficiency across the closely related Scandinavian tongues). He also notably translated works by the significant Yiddish writer Sholem Asch, frequently working from German intermediary versions, thus showcasing an engagement with another vital and rich strand of European literary and cultural heritage.

While translation formed the bedrock of his literary career and represents his most voluminous output, Paul Selver continued to pursue his own original creative writing throughout much of his life. He authored and published several novels, including *Schooling* (1924) and *Private Life* (1928). Although these original works have perhaps been somewhat overshadowed by the sheer scale and impact of his translations, they offer valuable insights into his personal literary preoccupations, his own narrative style, and the intellectual currents of his time. In addition to fiction, he also produced works of non-fiction, most notably the aforementioned critical study of Otakar Březina. His practical engagement with language also extended to the field of lexicography; he was involved in the compilation of dictionaries, including a widely used *Czech-English and English-Czech Pocket Dictionary*. This latter activity serves to underscore his deeply embedded, practical, and scholarly relationship with the languages he so expertly navigated.

Contemporary perceptions of Paul Selver would undoubtedly have acknowledged him as a linguist of exceptional skill and a literary craftsman of immense diligence and integrity. Within the prefaces, acknowledgements, and critical apparatus of his many translations, one frequently finds evidence of his meticulous approach to the translator's art. The very act of translating such a wide and challenging array of modernist and classical texts from less commonly taught languages was, in itself, a formidable achievement, particularly in the early to mid-twentieth century. He was operating in a period when literary translation was often a poorly remunerated and under-appreciated profession, yet his dedication remained unwavering, and his output was nothing short of prodigious. He functioned, in essence, as a vital cultural ambassador, patiently and skilfully facilitating a rich intellectual and artistic dialogue between Great Britain and the often turbulent, yet creatively fertile, nations of Central and Eastern Europe during the critical interwar years and well into the post-World War II era.

The challenges Selver confronted in his work would have been considerable. Securing reliable source texts, accessing comprehensive scholarly resources, and establishing direct contact with authors (though he is known to have corresponded with some, including Čapek) could often prove difficult, particularly in times of political instability. Moreover, the translator perpetually navigates the delicate tightrope between absolute fidelity to the source text and the imperative of creating a version that is natural, readable, and impactful in the target language. Selver consistently negotiated these inherent challenges with considerable adroitness, producing translations that were generally commended for their clarity, their literary merit, and their faithful reflection of the original author's intent and spirit. His prose style in translation was typically characterised by its lucidity and unpretentiousness, consistently aiming to serve the original author's voice rather than to superimpose his own stylistic idiosyncrasies too heavily upon the text.

Paul Selver continued his dedicated literary activities across many decades, his career spanning a period of immense historical, political, and cultural upheaval in Europe. He witnessed the cataclysmic rise and fall of ideologies, the painful redrawing of national borders, and the ever-shifting tides of literary fashion and critical taste. Yet, through all these vicissitudes, he remained a steadfast and productive presence, quietly and expertly facilitating the crucial movement of ideas, stories, and cultural understanding across the formidable, yet ultimately bridgeable, frontiers of language. He passed away on 6th April 1970, at the venerable age of 82, leaving behind an extraordinary legacy of cross-cultural enrichment.

His enduring legacy is that of a profoundly dedicated and exceptionally versatile man of letters who played an indispensable, if often unsung, role in broadening the literary horizons of the English-speaking world. For generations of readers encountering the unique and prophetic genius of Karel Čapek in English, Paul Selver's name remains inextricably linked with that formative experience of discovery. While Sir Nigel Playfair undoubtedly brought his invaluable theatrical flair and presentational acumen to the landmark London premiere of *R.U.R.*, it was Paul Selver who provided the essential linguistic key, meticulously unlocking Čapek's original Czech for a new and eager Anglophone audience. His extensive and consistently high-quality translations ensured that Čapek's profound humanism, his prescient anxieties about technology, and his incisive critiques of societal folly could resonate with power and clarity far beyond the geographical and linguistic borders of Czechoslovakia. Paul Selver stands as a distinguished and exemplary figure of the translator as an essential, though frequently under-celebrated, artist, scholar, and cultural intermediary, without whose tireless efforts world literature would undoubtedly be a far poorer, more fragmented, and less interconnected landscape. His life's work is a powerful testament to the profound and enduring importance of those who dedicate their lives to the intricate and noble art of carrying meaning across the beautiful, challenging, and endlessly fascinating divides of language.